THE GO-BETWEEN

A heart-warming tale of human and animal companionship

Life for Lou Barton since she lost her husband has been difficult. Living alone in an isolated cottage she feels her life is over, but everything changes when she finds a badly injured kitten on her way home after a dreadful day. Through him Lou is introduced to new friends, and the cat's empathy brings the little community together in ways that nobody – least of all Lou – could have expected.

Joyce Stranger titles available from Severn House Large Print

A GUIDING STAR

THE GO-BETWEEN

Joyce Stranger

Severn House Large Print
London & New York

This first large print edition published 2010
in Great Britain and the USA by
SEVERN HOUSE PUBLISHERS LTD of
9-15 High Street, Sutton, Surrey, SM1 1DF.
First world regular print edition published 2009 by
Severn House Publishers Ltd., London and New York.

British Library Cataloguing in Publication Data

Stranger, Joyce.
The go-between.
1. Widows--Fiction. 2. Cats--Fiction. 3. Human-animal relationships--Fiction. 4. Communities--Fiction. 5. Large type books.
I. Title
823.9'14-dc22

ISBN-13: 978-0-7278-7903-5

Severn House Publishers support The Forest Stewardship Council [FSC], the leading international forest certification organisation. All our titles that are printed on Greenpeace-approved FSC-certified paper carry the FSC logo.

Printed and bound in Great Britain by the
MPG Books Group, Bodmin, Cornwall.

This book is dedicated to my daughter Annie, without whom it would never have been finished, and in loving memory of my very dear mother, without whom it would never have been started.

Preface

In late September of 2007, Mum developed severe back pain. This was initially thought to be due to a collapsed vertebra, but sadly, in early December, tests revealed that she had advanced cancer. This book was very much on her mind and she wanted to finish it but was unable to do so. We talked together of how she wanted the book to end and agreed that I would finish it for her. Mum died peacefully at home on December 20th, enjoying watching the birds feeding outside her bedroom window, almost to the last. The pheasant, resplendent in his clerical collar, was a favourite and we laughed together about the fact that he obviously hadn't told his wives that there was a new feeding site at the front of the house!

There were eighteen chapters of the book in draft form and I found that, rather like a 'Painting by Numbers', the outline was there but much remained to be filled in, and in some places the picture was not quite complete. So, before I could finish it I had to do the colouring in and some redrawing. Within these pages there are many of Mum's original words, there are many of mine and there are many where I don't know where Mum ends and I begin. Which is, finally, as it should be and we hope that you, the readers, enjoy it!

Annie Noble, January, 2009

One

From a bird's eye view, the landscape unfolded like a patchwork quilt over the gentle undulations of hill and valley.

At its northern end, a broad stretch of motorway carried a steady stream of cars and lorries east and west. The black tarmac of a dual carriageway arrowed off the motorway to join a main road that ran from north to south. The town of Larksbridge sat firmly in the centre, an impersonal mixture of old buildings, new housing and a shopping mall. Nature had its way in the rest of the panorama: green field and brown earth, wooded copse and outcrops of grey rock splashed with yellow gorse, all divided by meandering lane and track, and the silver thread of stream and brook.

Down in the south-west corner, the lichened tower of Marshley's church rose from a clump of elm trees, noisy with rooks in summer. Beside the church, a narrow track meandered for half a mile. It was the only way to get to Lane End Farm where broken windows gaped in the farmhouse, most of the barn had collapsed and rotten doors hung from rusty hinges. Rats rustled in old hay, an owl nested in the barn and, in summer, swallows dipped and twisted for insects around the dilapidated buildings. A stream flowed around the edge of the farm, into a pond where ducks still dabbled, and out again to run under a humpback bridge in the village and beyond to the big river. On its way to the village, the curves of the stream marked the bottom boundaries of three gardens. The first of these, the one nearest Lane End Farm, was not much more than a field. Meadow flowers flourished in the long grass and weeds were rampant in the flower beds closer to the house. Shaggy pink poppies, marguerites and brilliant blue spikes of delphinium still managed to flower through the chaos. Two ancient willows flanked the stream, their exposed roots clinging to the flood-eroded banks so that the trees leaned at crazy angles and gave the house its name – Twisted Willows Cottage.

From here, the lane looped round again and another house nestled into the curve, separated from Twisted Willows Cottage by a thick hedge, ancient with holly and elderflower, bramble, hazel and hawthorn. Its name – The Bramble Patch – spoke of the builder's frustrations; its garden belied the name. Here, a row of old apple and pear trees stretched down to the stream. A cobbled path curved through neatly mown grass and on through the rough patch at the bottom of the garden where the stream flowed and a simple wooden bridge crossed it. Rhododendrons flourished beside the house and herbaceous borders blazed with colour throughout much of the year. From the branches of the fruit trees hung strings of nuts, fat balls and bird feeders. A patio graced the back of the house, a bird table beside it and a stone bird bath, pitted and weathered.

Beyond The Bramble Patch, the lane again turned to skirt around an outcrop of rock and another house tucked itself into the contours of the land. When the stream flooded its waters lapped halfway up the long, sloping garden, and so the house had been named Brookside. Another ancient hedgerow separated it from The Bramble Patch on one side and the rocky outcrop formed a natural boundary between it and the last house on the lane, opposite the church.

Bird and pheasant, rabbit, mole and other small furry creatures of the hedgerow wandered freely between the gardens, as had the humans who once lived there – when the farm was still alive, when blood and family, the common tie of working the land, had united the lane's inhabitants. Time, and the changes that came with it, had eroded the community as surely as the river eroded the land – each house and its occupant now an island.

In the north-eastern corner of the patchwork stood Stone's Throw Farm. Its Victorian builder had eccentrically named it because it was miles from anywhere. Now, though, with the invasion of the motorway, it was indeed a stone's throw from most places. In the warmer months of the year the cows trekked across the bridge connecting the divided farmland, pausing to gaze with astonished eyes at the strange things hurtling below, before treading ponderously along the track past the wood, across two fields and into the farmyard and milking parlour. Above them buzzards often soared, circling high and slow on the updraughts, descending to sit on the branch of a tree.

It was March and the sky was overcast, the air bitingly cold. Icicles hung from the eaves of the farmhouse and Liz Fletcher hurried across the yard from the milking parlour to the hen house tucked into the corner of the back garden. She was muffled up in thick jacket and trousers, her father's old flat cap pulled down as usual over a mass of curly hair. Her cheeks glowed red in the cold and her feet, even in thick socks and wellies, were frozen. Milking had been slow to start – the pipes frozen and in need of thawing. The cows had slipped and slithered on the hard, frosted yard, their breath steaming in the cold air. She had fed the calves and shutting up the hens for the night was her last outside job before she could relax into the warmth of the kitchen.

She tucked the last of the few eggs into the old pail and stamped back to the farmhouse, trying to bring some feeling into her toes. Benbow, the old, black tomcat, was eating his food outside the back door but there was no sign of Plush, the tabby. The last of the cows came out of the milking shed as she opened the back door. Mark yelled at the beast and slapped her on the rump, trying to hurry her up. That one was always trying to get back into the shed to get at the food the cows had whilst they were milked. She was cantankerous and greedy so they left her till last. It wouldn't be long before the menfolk were in for their teas and there was still the table to lay and the vegetables to put on to cook.

The kitchen was huge – black-beamed above and stone-flagged below. The range was tucked into a stone alcove where once a huge fire had blazed. In the middle of the room stood a large, square, wooden table, which had been at home in that same kitchen for a hundred years. It was battered, grooved where knives had cut, less than flat in places, and carried the history of generations. Breakfasts, lunch and in-between times, its grained and scrubbed surface was good enough but, at teatime, Liz liked to honour the meal with a tablecloth. She quickly thrust the pans of prepared vegetables on to the hot plates and pulled the cloth out of its drawer. The feathered tail of Haddock, the golden retriever, wagged gently against the floor from underneath the table.

Liz laughed and said, 'Are you hoping for extras, you greedy dog?'

His tail tapped harder against the stones

and he barked once, as though agreeing. Only he knew that Zannie, Liz's youngest daughter, sat cross-legged under the table with Plush, the farm tabby, on her lap. Haddock didn't mind sharing the space with a cat but there were those who would.

Liz bent to remove the last batch of bread buns from the range and slid them off on to a wire rack on the bench beside it. She had always loved baking. If it wasn't for the hard work of running the farm, she often said, she would weigh as much as an elephant, what with four children and all the cooking she did. Mark, her husband, described her as a perfect settee: well upholstered, curved in all the right places, soft yet supportive.

The back door opened, bringing a gust of cold air with it. Liz turned as Mark stepped into the kitchen and closed the door behind him. His huge frame was still clothed in the overalls he wore for milking, and he wore a bright, blue-and-white striped woollen hat pulled down over his ears – like a Cornish ware sugar bowl, Liz often said. Curls of brown hair escaped from underneath it.

Mark blew vigorously into his hands and clapped them into his armpits. 'I know, I know,' he said. 'I've not taken my milking clothes off yet. I just needed a warm before

I get cleaned up. It's that cold out there I had frost in my beard!' He leaned against the range and smiled. 'Oh, that's so nice. I've been looking forward to that.' Looking round the kitchen he asked, 'Where's Zannie? It's not like her to miss tea.'

Liz replied, 'I think she's upstairs. I'm sure she'll be down by the time you're ready to eat. Now, off you go and let me get at the oven. I can smell the cows with you warming yourself. It's spoiling the smell of the pie!'

By the time he emerged from the scullery, the food was on the table. Tom the cowman joined them, as he always did. He pulled out a chair and sat down, sighing with relief. 'Bye, it's a cold one today,' he said. 'I'm ready for a mug of tea to wrap my hands round.'

Liz poured from the big teapot, added milk and sugar and handed him the steaming mug. He took it and drank.

'That's strong enough to tan leather, sweet enough to ice a cake. Just the way I like it,' he said. He took another mouthful, swallowed and glanced across at Zannie's empty chair. 'Where's the little lass?' he asked. 'Not poorly, is she?'

Mark looked across at Liz and asked, 'Is

she all right? She's still not appeared then?'

Liz frowned. 'I can't think where she can be. Last time I saw her she was playing with the cats in the yard.'

Under the table, Zannie stroked Plush's soft fur. She had taken pity on the animal, outside in that horrible cold weather, and decided to give her a treat. The cat purred loudly.

'Shhh!' said Zannie and held her breath, hand over mouth, hoping her father would not have heard.

It was too late.

The corner of the tablecloth lifted and he scowled down at her. She hunched over the cat, one arm curled protectively around the animal, and peeked up at him through blonde hair that tumbled in curls around her face. He pushed his chair back and squatted on the floor. Haddock stood up and barked, thinking it was a game. Zannie wanted to escape but there was nowhere to go, chair legs caging her. Mark pushed her arm away, grabbed Plush roughly by the scruff of her neck and pulled her out.

Plush dangled, unable to protest, as he rose to his feet and strode towards the back door shouting, 'I don't know how many times I've told you, Zannie. Cats do not belong in the house. Dogs, yes; cats, no.'

Zannie crawled out, climbing over Haddock, who had crept further under the table. She pushed a chair aside and ran after Mark shouting, 'You'll hurt her, Daddy!' She caught him up, pulled at his sleeve and begged, 'Stop it, you'll hurt her!'

He ignored her pleas, flung the back door open and threw the cat outside.

Zannie rushed after her, sobbing, 'It's too cold outside, Daddy. She'll die.'

Mark grabbed her by the arm and shouted, 'Go and sit down and eat your tea. I'm fed up with this.'

The cat crouched for a moment in the yard, her ears back and her fur standing on end. She swore once, low and angry, and then ran off.

Zannie stormed back inside, yelling at the top of her voice, 'I hate you, Daddy, and I don't want any tea.' She dashed upstairs, tears streaming down her face.

Liz and Tom looked at each other and sighed. Mark came back in, picked the chair up and sat down. 'Don't say anything, you two. Let's just have some food.'

Liz glared at him and said, 'How can you be so obstinate, Mark? It's only a cat.'

He glared back. 'It's tradition, Liz. It's

tradition that has kept this family here for all these years, it's tradition that keeps us going and part of that tradition is –' he paused and brought his fist down on the table with each word so that plates bounced, cutlery fell to the floor and Haddock emerged and went to lean against Liz's leg for comfort – 'cats – belong – outside. Cats – are – here – to – catch – mice.'

Liz sighed. It might as well be carved on the gable stone, under the date: 1861 – No Cats Allowed.

The salt cellar had fallen over, leaving a puddle of salt on the cloth. Mark reached across to throw a pinch of it over his left shoulder. It was the final straw.

Liz yelled, 'That's it, isn't it? It's your stupid superstitions. You –' she stabbed at him with her finger, her normally placid face tight with fury – 'are worse than an old woman. To think that I once thought they were funny!'

It was true. It was one of the things that had attracted her to him. It was pure chance they had met, moving, as they did, in such different worlds. But he had come to her university, with a group of students from the local agricultural college, to hear a lecture given by a well-known scientist about the rainforests. They had met up afterwards and talked – him awestruck by the wonders of the world he lived in, her first attracted by the size and look of him, and then by his mind and his enthusiasm for the farm that would be his some time in the future. At some point they had fallen in love. That such a practical man, such a handsome man, should turn his money at the new moon, always go in and out of the same door and never walk under a ladder, was a source of wonder, an endearing quality.

Yet it was true, too, that the things you loved in someone were also the things you hated. And when it was a cause of such antagonism – where was the sense in that? But he was as steeped in the lore and superstitions of country folk as was the house in its history. Horses might have given way to tractors, scythes to combine harvesters and lanes to motorways but some things never changed. It was as Mark said; the farm and the life of the farm were built on tradition.

Two

Liz sighed, and dropped the last peeled potato into the pan. Through the window she saw Zannie plodding across the garden yet again, calling repeatedly, 'Plush? Plush?' She bent to look under a shrub and then stood and circled, looking round anxiously.

Ten days on and Plush still hadn't returned.

Zannie blamed her father; quite rightly, Liz thought. Every day the child went from barn to stable, from the bull's pen to the milking parlour, looking for Plush in all of the cat's favourite places. Liz, too, was heartbroken – fearing for the safety of the cat and missing her presence.

Whilst there was also Benbow, and a couple of other cats that were so wild they never came near the house, Plush was Liz's favourite cat. How could she survive? The cold weather had continued; icicles grew longer, there was a crust of ice at the edges of the stream, and the water trough and earth were frozen solid. Today was the first time the sun had put in an appearance for days. It shone out of a clear, blue sky and the icicles were beginning to drip.

The last of the mountain of potatoes peeled, Liz took the pan across to the range and put it on the hob. She was tired of the strain of keeping the peace between father and daughter, tired of regret. They would have to replace the tabby if she didn't come back. Old, black Benbow couldn't keep the vermin down by himself and, without Plush, there would be no more kittens. Between them, she and Benbow had had several litters. They were both grand mousers and Plush had the temperament of a teddy bear, even though she was an outside cat. Their offspring were in high demand and there always seemed to be someone eagerly inquiring when the next litter might be expected. Liz wiped a tear away, thinking there might be no more.

Then she heard Zannie's voice outside and the back door banged against the wall as her daughter rushed in, shouting, 'Mummy, Plush has come back! She's in the greenhouse!'

Liz spun round to look at her, unbelieving at first.

Zannie said excitedly, 'It's true, Mum, really true. Come and see.'

She tugged her by the hand and Liz followed her out into the back garden and across to the greenhouse, which stood next to the hen enclosure. Sure enough there was Plush, curled up in the potting tray in a puddle of sunshine, purring gently.

Liz smiled and scratched Plush's head. Plush purred more loudly and rolled over to have her tummy rubbed, waving her paws in the air.

'Thank goodness!' Liz said to Zannie. 'I was really afraid we were never going to see her again.' She looked down at her small daughter and asked, 'Are you going to forgive Daddy now?'

Zannie kicked at the edge of a paving slab. She frowned and scratched Plush between her ears. Then she looked up and giggled. 'Of course I am. I expect she's been on holiday, like we did last year.'

Three weeks later, Tom came into the kitchen at teatime and said, 'I reckon that cat's eating too much. She's fatter than she was when she went off!'

Liz went out to look at her. She bent to stroke Plush as the cat ate from the old saucer. She had certainly gained weight since she came back, but then she had needed to. Plush sat and licked round her whiskers, making sure she had missed nothing, and then licked a paw and rubbed it over her face. Satisfied, she stood, stretched each back leg and trotted back to the barn.

Tom appeared at the back door and watched her go. 'I reckon she's pregnant,' he said.

'Hmm,' said Liz, 'I wonder...' The cat disappeared into the barn and she continued, 'I wonder if she found a mate while she was away?'

'Happen she did,' said Tom. 'There're plenty of possibilities around.'

Liz grinned and said, 'It'll be interesting to see what the kittens are like if Benbow isn't the father.'

Tom grunted, 'They'll be the same as usual I expect: black, tabby, ginger or piebald. Cats are cats, whatever the dad.'

Liz knew that Plush's time was near when the cat took to sleeping in the stable instead of on the potting bench in the greenhouse. Marnie, Liz's old grey mare, huffed at Plush in the evening as she munched her hay and kept the cat company. The mare accepted her presence, and Plush knew that Marnie's hooves could not reach her where she lay, curled in a nest of fallen hay behind the manger. The place was warm and quiet and she always had her kittens there.

Zannie was sitting at the kitchen table drawing when Liz returned from one early morning visit to the stable. It was a warm spring day; white blossom was beginning to break in the hedgerows and the first leaves were unfolding, fresh and green.

A newly opened packet of felt-tip pens lay amongst the debris of breakfast, birthday cards and wrapping paper. A big, red balloon with a number five on it floated from the back of Zannie's chair and she wore a crown made of golden foil. There was a sticky patch of marmalade on her picture and she was trying to lick it off.

'Look what I've done, Mummy,' she grumbled. 'I dropped my toast on it and it landed the wrong way up.'

'Never mind, Zannie, we can clean it later. Come and see what Plush has done for the birthday girl!'

Zannie jumped up and dashed out of the kitchen, still wearing her pyjamas. She thrust her bare feet into her wellies in the porch and raced across the yard to the stable.

'Slow down, Zannie!' Liz shouted. 'You'll frighten her!'

Zannie stopped and waited, slipping her hand into Liz's. Together they crept into the stable, skirted round the horse and peeped over the manger. Marnie ignored them, busy with her breakfast. Zannie caught her breath. Plush lay in the hay, stretched on her side, vigorously licking a newborn kitten. Three more squirmed blindly against her fur, searching for milk, their tiny, pink paws already kneading.

'They're so small,' she whispered. 'Hardly any bigger than Plush's paws!'

Plush released the latest one, its striped fur already drying. It wriggled determinedly over its litter mates, searching for food. Purring, Plush lay down again and draped a maternal paw over the nearest kitten.

'I think that might be it,' said Liz, just as Plush sat suddenly and birthed another kitten. Once again she licked vigorously, the kitten hidden. It wriggled into view and Zannie stared in astonishment.

'It looks a bit like one of those rats Simon used to keep, Mum!' Zannie said.

Pink-nosed, whip-tailed and completely white, the kitten submitted to the rough licking of its mother's tongue. Its siblings, all tabbies, looked as if they belonged in a different litter.

'It certainly does,' said Liz. 'I hope its looks improve! Isn't it smaller than the others? I wonder if it's all right.'

Zannie clutched her mother's hand. 'It is. I know it is. It's my favourite because I'm the smallest too, aren't I? It's going to be my cat. Please can it be my birthday cat: a present for me from Plush? Perhaps Daddy will change his mind now! It's so cute ... even if it does look like a rat at the moment.'

Liz looked down at her eager face, framed with its halo of blonde curls. In her heart she knew what the answer would be. She had fought her own battle over having Plush as a house pet and lost. Now she sensed trouble ahead.

Without answering the question, she said, 'Come on, Zannie. Let's go and get Plush some food. She'll be hungry after all her hard work. And, remember, we have a party to get ready for tonight!'

Zannie smiled. 'Are Simon, Billy and Sara all going to be there?'

'Of course they are! None of your big brothers and sisters would want to miss your birthday, would they?'

'Wheeeee!' yelled Zannie, running in circles round Liz. 'I can't wait! What's my cake going to be like?'

'That's for me to know and you to guess. Now, off you go and get dressed!'

Liz was looking forward so much to the party. It seemed ages since all the children had been home at the same time. She laughed at her thoughts. None of them except Zannie counted as children any more and they had all left home. There was Sara, the oldest, then Bill-in-the-middle, and finally Simon, the youngest of the three. Fifteen years after his birth, Liz had found she was pregnant. She smiled, remembering Simon's outrage.

'Mum, how could you?' he'd shouted, as though she were entirely to blame. He'd clutched at his unruly mop of hair and made her feel even worse than she already did by saying, 'Yuk! What will my friends think? You're way too old to have a baby.'

She'd said, with a laugh she hadn't quite felt, 'That's what we thought too.'

Bill had been sitting at the kitchen table, his head down on his arms. He'd looked up with an anguished expression and moaned, 'There go my A levels. I'll never get any work done. It'll be "yell, yell, yell" all the time.'

Only Sara had been pleased. 'Ooh, maybe I'll have a sister,' she'd said with a big smile.

The boys had turned on her, utter horror on their faces, saying in chorus, 'Oh no! Not another girl!'

Sara's response had been to swipe them both with the wet tea towel she was holding and they had both run screaming from the kitchen.

It had been the first kicks of the baby that had brought acceptance, which had been followed by impatience and excitement. They had watched Liz's huge bump with fascination, putting a cup of water on it when she lay resting on the settee in the evening and placing bets as to whether or not the baby would manage to kick it off. How they had laughed when it did, soaking Liz in the process.

She hadn't dared to buy anything until her due date was near, made nervous by her age. Then they had all rushed out together one Saturday to get 'The Baby Kit' as Simon called it.

The name had been much discussed. The boys had pretended disgust when they found out it was a girl, and then both gone out to buy pink teddies. It was Bill who had come up with Zannie, and everyone had loved it.

What a delightful baby Zannie had been. Placidly sleeping when she should, eating anything that came her way and smiling and waving little fists and feet at anybody who stopped to play. She had had a fan club of three from day one; instant love had been on all their faces as they gazed down at her. Sara had reluctantly returned to university, coming home nearly every weekend that first year. Bill had sailed through his A levels and left for university himself when Zannie was two. And Simon had gone last year, much to Zannie's disgust. She had pleaded with him to stay, hung on to his legs when he went out to the car to be driven away and had cried for an afternoon when he had finally gone.

So Zannie was always exuberant when she knew they were coming home. Liz felt sad for her daughter sometimes, who'd missed out on the hurly-burly of family life when siblings were close in age.

But there.

These things happened and it was no good wishing.

'Come on, Zannie! Time for school,' Liz shouted from the foot of the stairs. The words were strange. Was she really that age already? There was no answer and, when Liz went to look, Zannie's bedroom was empty. Where was the child? They didn't want to be late on her first day.

She hurried back downstairs and looked under the table. Not in her usual hiding place either. There was one more place she might be.

Liz hurried across the yard and into the stable. Zannie lay on her tummy under the manger watching the kittens.

'There you are!' Liz cried. 'We need to hurry for school. Look at you. Not even dressed yet.'

'Do I have to go today, Mum?' asked Zannie. 'Won't tomorrow do instead?'

'No, it won't. You've been looking forward to this for ages – your first day!'

'I know, but that was before the kittens...' She looked longingly at them as they fed.

Plush mewed softly and Liz bent to stroke her. Standing, she said firmly, 'Plush won't want you here all the time, Zannie. She needs some peace and quiet. They'll still be here tonight.'

'OK.' Zannie sighed, scrambling to her feet.

After that, every day was the same. Zannie

was either in the stable or at school.

At first, all the kittens did was eat and sleep, but she loved to watch them struggle over each other in their search for the best place to feed. Her favourite – already 'my kitten' in her mind – was pushy and determined to get exactly where it wanted to be. Every day she came in with a bulletin for her mother and, a few days after her birthday, she was entranced to find the kittens' eyes were opening.

Not only were her kitten's eyes open, revealing a brilliant blue, but there were darker patches appearing on his white fur. It was as though smoke had drifted around his tail, paws and face, leaving a smudge of ash behind. 'He doesn't look like a rat any more, Mum,' she said.

Liz was fascinated too, especially by Zannie's favourite. 'I'm beginning to think the impossible happened and Plush found a very aristocratic daddy for this lot,' she said, when they were about three weeks old. 'Your favourite looks as if he is pure Siamese!' The light-grey smudges had darkened to greyish-brown on ears, nose, paws and tail; his eyes were still the blue of speedwells. Liz had to agree that he was beautiful. Even Tom was entranced, but Mark remained unimpressed.

Later that evening Liz talked about it with Tom. 'I wonder if Plush's mother managed to mate with one of those Siamese from up the road,' she said, 'and Plush followed in her mother's footsteps when Mark threw her out.'

'Happen she did,' said Tom. 'You can get unexpected surprises with cows, so I suppose you can with cats. She had an exotic holiday, apparently!'

Zannie loved watching them trying to wash. Their legs were still unsteady as they wobbled through the hay and Plush kept a careful eye on them. They rolled around and batted at one another, and then suddenly fell asleep in a furry mound of twitching ears and tails. If Liz couldn't find Zannie, she always knew where she would be.

By the time five weeks had passed, nearly all the new kittens had homes to go to. Privately, Liz was hoping that someone would fall in love with Zanny's favourite but his voice always put them off. Whereas the other kittens mewed gently, and not that often, he yowled, his noise a constant, loud commentary on the world he found himself in. It was obvious now that he took after his Siamese father and everybody knew the noise that Siamese cats could make! If he sounded like that at five weeks what on earth would he be like as an adult? Also it was obvious that Zannie doted on him, and the prospective buyers weren't willing to take what looked like Zannie's pet from her.

To the kitten, though, people meant conversation. There was so much to tell them!

'Good grief,' they would say. 'We can't live with that!'

Mark knew that Zannie wanted the kitten to be hers but he ignored her pleas. Liz waited anxiously for matters to come to a head and, sure enough, they did. She was shutting the hens up for the night when she heard loud wails of distress from the kitchen. She rushed in to find Zannie, crying her eyes out, and Mark, red in the face and furious. Zannie was clutching the kitten to her chest.

'I want him to start sleeping on my bed, Mummy, and Daddy says he can't. He says he's not to come in the house and I've got to put him back in the stable now.' She stamped her foot, and shouted, 'But I won't! I don't see why he can't. It's not fair!' Her look was desperate as she pleaded, 'You as good as promised, Mummy.'

Liz stared at her and said, 'No, I didn't promise, Zannie. I couldn't. We both know Daddy won't have cats in the house. He really isn't going to change his mind.' She wondered what had happened to the placid child Zannie had once been, thinking that her daughter was as stubborn in her own way as her father was in his.

Zannie stuck out her lower lip and scowled. 'Well, you nearly promised and I want to give him a proper name. Daddy says I can't because his new owners will choose a name. But I want him to stay here and be my "forever" cat.'

Liz sighed. 'Listen, Zannie. Put him out with Plush for now. None of the kittens have left her yet. They aren't old enough. Put him back and go to bed. I'll talk to Daddy for you.'

She tried again later that night after Mark came in from the milking and sat eating his tea, a can of beer beside him. 'Can't she keep him, Mark? It's only one little kitten and it will be company for her. She hasn't often got other children to play with at home and she's set her heart on that little fellow. Nobody else seems to want him.'

He drained the can of beer and banged it down, wiped froth from his moustache with the back of his hand and said, 'No. That's the end of the matter. Cats and humans should not be under the same roof.'

Liz plunged on, aware of danger from his expression but determined to fight Zannie's corner. 'But why not? Isn't it about time to end that old fairy tale? It's just superstition. Isn't the happiness of your daughter more important than keeping some old family nonsense going?'

He stood up, pushing his half-empty plate to one side. He spoke, every word measured, feeling like a blow to Liz. 'Nonsense it might be but I don't intend to change my mind. I have my reasons. Good heavens, Liz, do you take me for a fool?'

Liz stood up and swept the rest of his food into the dog's bowl. 'At this moment, yes, I do think you're a fool. An illogical fool who cares more about the past than the future.'

Upstairs a door slammed and Zannie, from the top of the stairs, yelled, 'I hate you, Daddy.' The friction between them seemed never ending.

Tom stood up and stretched. As usual he wore an old boiler suit. Its buttons were long gone and the sides kept together with a tattered length of orange binder twine tied round his waist. He said, 'Come on, Mark.

There's a cow needs looking at. I think she may calve tonight.' He winked at Liz and she raised her eyebrows and sighed.

Outside, the two men sat on straw bales in the cowshed and discussed the beast. Her yellow ear tag said she was number forty-seven but her real name was Roo. Zannie had named the whole herd after characters from her favourite books and she knew each one of them by name. Every beast that lived on the farm since she could talk had been christened by her fertile imagination. The family used to laugh at her choices and Liz had once joked, 'I expect she'll call her own children Toad and Ratty.'

'I don't often challenge you, Mark,' said Tom, 'but I'm going to this time. You know how she loves the animals and loves to name them. She hasn't got one to call her own and Liz is right. She's desperate to keep the kitten.'

'Don't you start. It's bad enough having those two on at me.'

'What are you afraid of? He's only a little scrap of fur. He's toilet-trained now and would be fine in the house.'

Mark stirred the hay with the toe of his boot, a scowl on his face. He would not look Tom in the eye. Then he glanced up and muttered, 'They're unlucky.'

Tom grinned. 'You don't really believe that superstitious nonsense, do you? Come on, this is the twenty-first century. Witches and black cats went out of fashion years ago.'

'I don't care. It's what I was brought up on. Cats in the house bring death. Every generation of my family that has lived in this house has stories to tell about the bad luck and tragedies that have been brought about by cats. It's not safe to tempt fate. Heaven knows there are enough things to go wrong. It might be nonsense but I am not taking the risk. I have too much to lose. Cats exist to catch rats and mice. That's final!'

Mark stood and dusted the hay off the seat of his trousers and went out to lean on the gate and look at the stars. In the manger, the unwanted kitten stretched and yowled in his sleep. As though he had other ideas.

Three

The kitten pranced sideways out of the stable door, his back arched and tail bushed. Moving objects existed to be hunted. He leapt for Haddock's front paw and attacked, small teeth biting, back legs kicking. The dog stopped and lay down, and the kitten rolled over on his back between his front paws, batting at his nose. The last of his litter mates had gone and he missed them. His mother didn't want to play or explore like they had.

Plush still anxiously watched him. A foray out of the yard, into the garden or the field and she was after him. Liz often looked out to see Plush heading determinedly back to the stable with an indignantly protesting scrap hanging from her jaws. Once there she would drop him, pin him down with a paw and set to work with her tongue – licking him into submission. It never lasted long. 'The world is too exciting to be in here,' he would protest loudly while wriggling free and scampering out again.

Haddock, new playmate and guardian, never seemed far away. The dog, watching Zannie pull a string for the kitten to chase, learned to do the same. Liz screamed with laughter one day at the sight of Haddock in the yard with a length of baler twine in his mouth. He walked in a circle, head down and ears flopping, an indulgent expression on his face as he watched the little animal pounce and chase.

There was no mystery in knowing where the kitten was. Tom, listening to him yowling outside the kitchen one day, turned to Liz and said, 'Eh, that young one's a *catter*box if ever there was one!' Liz hooted with laughter and Tom went on, 'I don't think he's paused for breath in the last five minutes. I've never heard anything like it. He's driving Mark crazy.'

'I'm sure he's talking to us,' said Liz.

To the kitten, the world was indeed a wonderful place and he wanted everybody to know exactly what he thought about it. He had no sense of danger at all.

'Tom? Tom?' called Zannie as he stomped across the yard wiping sweat from his face. The sun had blazed down all day and it was still swelteringly hot. July had finally brought summer with it. 'He's done it again,' said Zannie.

'That blessed cat. It's the sixth time today.' He fetched the ladder, which he no longer bothered to put away, and Zannie followed him into the barn.

The kitten, perched high on a cross-beam, gazed down at them with wide, blue eyes. He yowled pathetically, 'I'm stuck. Help! Get me down.'

Tom clambered up the ladder and retrieved him. The kitten perched on his shoulder as he descended, balancing precariously and exclaiming about his adventure. As soon as Tom's feet touched ground, the kitten scrambled down.

'Aye, you can manage that easily enough,' said Tom.

Before Zannie could pick him up another swallow flew into the barn and up towards the roof. The kitten leapt for the pillar and clawed himself back to the top. The swallow flew out of the door and the kitten raced across the beam after it. At the other end, he stopped and yowled excitedly, 'Isn't this a good game? Fetch me down again!'

Tom wagged a finger at him. 'I've a good mind to leave you up there. You're a perfect pest!'

'Meeow!' said the kitten in agreement.

'I'm going to call him Flyer,' said Zannie. 'That's what he does – he flies up there to be with the swallows.'

'I don't think it's so much to *be* with as to eat!' said Tom.

It was two weeks later when disaster threatened. In the shed beyond the stable lived the huge bull. He was generally an affable fellow, known as Old Codger, though Zannie had named him Semolina. Liz and Mark thought this was because of his creamy colour; they were wrong! The pudding had once been forced upon her at school and she lived in dread of the horrible stuff appearing again. Her feelings about it were much the same as those she had about the bull so it had seemed to her a perfectly sensible name for the massive beast.

Old Codger bellowed and his feet thudded against the door. It crashed open and he stormed out into the yard, bucking wildly. On his back, claws firmly anchored, rode Flyer. His tightening grip maddened the bull even more – the sharp claws were an agony and an insufferable indignation. Tom rushed to shut the gates to keep him in the yard, and shooed Zannie into the house.

Zannie sobbed, 'Flyer's going to die, Mum, he's going to die. Semolina will kill him.'

Liz soothed her, saying, 'No, he's not. Tom will sort it.'

Tom yelled, 'Fetch me some beer in a bucket, will you?' as he skirted round the yard. Old Codger stood in the middle, exhausted, and Flyer released his grip. Feeling movement the bull bucked again and threw Flyer from his back. The kitten arced through the air to land with a splash in the horse trough. He disappeared under the water and surfaced, scrabbling wildly for the side. Tom hauled him out by his scruff and threw him in the stable, closing the door firmly on the wailing animal.

Liz slipped across with the bucket and Tom rattled it gently, speaking softly.

'OK, Old Codger, OK. He's gone now. You're safe. Come on, come and have your pint.'

The bull snorted and came to sink his nose into the bucket.

'There you go,' said Tom and led the beast back to his shed.

Flyer yelled from the stable, 'Come and get me. I'm wet. I'm frightened. I want company.'

'You're nothing but trouble!' shouted Tom through the closed door and then went in to fetch him. He took the bedraggled animal in to Zannie and said, 'You'd better wrap him in a towel and dry him. Your dad's off in town still so you should be OK for a while.'

Zannie took him and he purred and then began to tell her all about it.

'Phew, I need a cuppa after that,' said Tom.

'Me too,' said Liz. 'I was terrified. I was sure the cat would die, the bull would escape and you would be gored!'

Tom grinned. 'All's well that ends well. I hardly had time to think, it happened so quickly. But how many lives has he lost now?'

Liz thought and said, 'I've lost count. I reckon it's five. There was the time he went to sleep under the wheel arch of the Land Rover and it was only because Haddock warned us that we found him before I drove off.'

'There was the time he chased a frog and followed it into the pond.'

'The stray dog that nearly got him.'

'Aye, he's used to ours playing with him. He certainly didn't expect to be dog fodder.'

'I've never seen him run so fast! And then he shot to the top of the apple tree and needed rescuing from there.'

'Never known a cat like him,' said Tom.

'I've just remembered another one,' said Liz. 'That time he crept into the washing machine in the scullery and nearly got put on to hot wash. If it hadn't been for his indignant yowl when I threw in a pair of Mark's socks he would have been a goner.'

'Perhaps it's a good job that he is so talkative. It certainly saves his skin sometimes.'

Zannie was devoted to Flyer; the argument about his future was in uneasy abeyance. It did not make for a comfortable atmosphere in the house.

The kitten cared nothing for the future.

As the days passed, a conspiracy developed between Liz and Zannie. There were often times when Mark was off about farm business, and then Flyer was brought into the kitchen to play. He loved to curl up and sleep by the stove, chase a piece of string, dribble a small ball of paper round the legs of the kitchen table and invent intricate ways of getting round the under frame of a chair. He loved to climb the curtains, to look for mice hiding in the middle of cardboard rolls and to slide under the rug in front of the fire. He loved to climb up people, and often hauled himself up their clothes to perch on their heads like a vociferous, furry, Russian hat.

But Zannie's lap was his favourite place. When she was feeling sad or lonely, grumpy or tired, he would pat at her leg and jump on to her lap to purr and rub his head against her hand. On her return from school each day he was ecstatic. He would sit by the gate watching for the Land Rover that brought her home. As she jumped out of the back door, a slow, rumbling purr would start, deep in his throat, rising to exuberant yowls of joy as he raced towards her and jumped to her shoulder. There he would rub his head contentedly against her face and reach a paw to tap her on the mouth, as if insisting that she tell him about her day too. She would drop her school bag, fold her arms and he would leap into them and submit to an equally exuberant hug. It was his way of saying 'I missed you'. Then Zannie would look round and ask, 'Where's Dad?' knowing that if he was out of the way Flyer could come into the house with her.

Liz didn't like it, but neither did she like the feeling of having to take sides with her husband against her daughter. It was a problem that would have to be solved somehow, but meanwhile perhaps he might still change his mind. Thinking about it, she sniffed and muttered, 'Huh! When the moon turns blue, perhaps.'

Liz and Zannie were sitting eating lunch one Saturday when the back door slowly opened and they looked up to see Sara standing in the doorway.

Liz jumped to her feet. 'What on earth are you doing here? I thought you were in London this weekend, shopping for the house.'

Sara burst into tears and Liz realized that her eyes were already red and swollen. She hugged her daughter close as Sara wept and finally managed to say, 'That is what I was going to do but I've lost my job. I can't afford anything now. The lease on my flat has run out and Paul has finished with me. Oh, Mum, what am I going to do? I have no job, nowhere to live and no boyfriend. I can't bear it.'

'Come on, love. Sit down. Have a cuppa and tell me about it.'

Sara pulled out a chair opposite Zannie and sat. She yelped as sharp claws pierced her trousers. She looked under the table and hauled out the kitten. Holding the little scrap of fur up to her face, she managed a smile. 'Hello! Are you that little, white kitten born on Zannie's birthday? Aren't you gorgeous!'

'That's Flyer,' said Zannie. 'He's a secret in the house. Daddy mustn't see him.'

Sara settled him down on her lap and stroked him. He began to purr and she put a finger to her lips saying, 'Mum's the word!'

Liz put a mug of coffee on the table in front of her and sat down. The story came out gradually as Sara, soothed by the purrs of the small creature, related the events of the past month. It was a sorry tale and, privately, Liz thought that Sara had probably had a lucky escape. How much harder it would have been if she already had the house. She had been trying since she first heard rumours of her redundancy to get another job but without success.

'Can I stay here, Mum, while I sort myself out?'

'Of course you can, darling. Where else would you go?'

The back door opened again and Mark walked in demanding, 'Whose bags are these outside?' He took in the sight of Liz, Sara and Zannie, saw the tears and then the kitten. Before anyone could explain he snapped, 'See? Trouble! Cat in house, women in tears. What's going on?'

Liz jumped to her feet. 'It has nothing to do with the cat, you stupid man. How can a cat in the house here make things happen to Sara in London?'

Mark shouted, 'And when did that animal first come in the house, may I ask? Now get it out!' He didn't wait to hear any explanations.

Zannie scooped up the kitten from Sara's lap and ran outside with him. Flyer, frightened by the raised voices and feeling the anger in the air, wriggled out of her arms and ran off to the safety of the barn. Zannie followed him sadly, knowing that his days in the house were over. She curled up beside him, tucking him into the crook of her arm and weeping quietly. She finally dozed, exhausted by her tears. Sara found them both there when supper was ready.

Sara knelt and gently shook Zannie awake. 'Come on, sweetheart. Tea's ready. Come in and wash your face.' She smiled. 'We both look a sight, don't we? It'll be all right. Mum's had a word with Dad and he won't say anything to you. Just keep Flyer outside for a while. We can always see him outside, can't we?'

Zannie struggled to her feet and patted him. 'Night, night. See you tomorrow,' she whispered. He curled up more tightly, his nose tucked under one paw. Sara took her hand and they walked back to the house.

After that it was a toss up who would be with Flyer. His instincts sensed Sara's unhappiness and he often sought out her company as she wandered round the farm. Her favourite place was down by the river, where she would sit on a log and watch the water flowing over the stones for hours. At first Zannie felt resentful, but then one day she saw Sara sobbing her heart out as she sat. Flyer trotted up to her and patted her on the leg, asking to be picked up. Sara smiled and scooped him on to her lap. His purrs rose into the air and Sara's sobs quieted.

Zannie crept away to draw a picture.

A picture of sunshine and flowers, and blue sky and birds; of a little house with smoke coming out of its chimney and a cat sitting on the doorstep. She framed it with kisses and slipped it under Sara's bedroom door that night.

Sara kept the picture under her pillow and slowly her mood lifted as she began to see light at the end of the tunnel. The rest of the family heaved sighs of relief as she began to make plans for a different future.

In the yard, a large cardboard box covered in baling plastic sat in one corner. A big label announced ‘Zannie’s House’ in crooked writing. Between them, Sara and Zannie had dragged the box from the scullery, laid an old piece of carpeting inside and furnished it with cushions, blanket, a small table and an old milking stool.

‘You’re allowed in here,’ Zannie announced proudly to Flyer and disappeared inside with the kitten, closing the makeshift door behind them. From inside she called, ‘It’s very dark! I can’t see anything!’

Sara cut a window in the side and taped clear plastic across it for her.

‘Perfect,’ sighed Zannie, and Flyer, digging between the cushions with a small, brown paw, just in case there was a mouse down there, agreed.

When Zannie returned to school in September he made her house his headquarters, and when she returned from school he was always ready to greet her in his usual exuberant way. At weekends she insisted on eating her breakfast and lunch ‘in my own house,’ she said, ‘with my own cat.’

* * *

A northerly wind moaned round the farm buildings under a dark, cloud-filled sky. Bits of straw blew across the yard and doors rattled in their frames. It excited Flyer, bringing tantalizing drifts of new smells, making his blood flow strong in his veins. He jumped on to the garden wall and then out into the field.

The grass had been cut for silage and there was no cover for him. He went quickly, tail high and ears pricked, trotting across the field towards the distant wood. Nobody saw him go – Zannie was sitting on the stool in her house with a book, Liz and Sara were collecting eggs, and Tom and Mark were with the cows. Only the buzzard, sitting on the branch of a tree, noticed the moving flash of pale fur. He took flight.

In the middle of the second field Flyer crouched suddenly, aware of danger. A rush of wings, a shadow and Flyer was running for his life. The buzzard dropped lower and Flyer swerved and raced again for cover. The buzzard, remorseless and hungry, followed him. The farm was far behind. No stone walls, no hedges into which he could dive and hide. Only barbed wire and fence post, and the distant promise of sanctuary in the wood.

No time to shout, no mother to rescue him, no Zannie. Nothing except his own resources.

The wood loomed closer with trees to climb and thickets of bramble to crawl into, away from the death danger of the pursuing bird.

A nettle stung him on the nose; the thorn of a trailing branch tore his ear, making blood well along the cut. He dived for cover, pushing his way through the tangle of branches. He stopped, his flanks heaving as he fought for breath. His ears flattened; his fur stood on end. He wanted to shout for help but he knew that any noise he made would betray him and, for once, he was quiet.

He longed for the farm, for all that was familiar, and once he had recovered his breath he pushed his way out of the thicket to make for home and safety.

The buzzard still waited. Frustrated by the escape of his prey, he had settled on a nearby branch. The rustle of dry leaves and a moving twig alerted him and he turned his head quickly. He took flight as Flyer emerged from the shelter of the undergrowth; low over the kitten, he dropped his legs. His talons pierced Flyer's shoulders and the kitten screamed in agony and terror. The buzzard rose slowly upwards, wing beats strong and slow, carried on the wind. Flyer screamed again.

Zannie dashed out of her house, terrified by the noise. Across the field she saw the buzzard. It was too far to see what he was carrying but the scream told her the truth. Tom rushed from the cowshed and Liz, dropping all the eggs, ran into the field waving her arms and yelling at the top of her voice. Zannie rushed past, screaming and distraught. The buzzard disappeared behind a low hill. He was gone, no hope of rescue. Liz and Sara ran to Zannie and held her close, all of them weeping helplessly.

There was nothing to be done. Flyer was gone.

Zannie was inconsolable. 'He's dead. I know he's dead, Mummy.'

She had nightmares – seeing the buzzard lift Flyer, trying to rescue him.

Mark had said, 'I told you so!' only once. Liz took herself off to the spare bedroom for a week. She relented only when she came into the kitchen one day to find Zannie sitting on his knee. He was telling her of how cats had nine lives. 'Flyer,' he said, using the cat's name for the first time, 'had used up some of his lives – but not all of them. He was a fine cat and I'm sure he's not dead. He still had some lives left. He might not be with us any more but I think he's with someone else now. Why don't you get your pens and make a picture of where he might be?'

When Liz went to say goodnight Zannie was sitting in bed looking at the picture she had drawn. A cream and brown cat was curled up on a rug in front of a fire. There was a saucer of milk and a plate of food beside him. A woman with bright-red hair sat in a chair reading a book.

Liz sat down on the bed and asked, 'Where do you think he is then?'

'The lady is looking after him, somewhere,' said Zannie. 'I expect Daddy's right and Flyer has a new home. I expect he's allowed in the house all the time and there're lots of people for him to talk to. I expect he's fine and he's still got some lives left.' She snuggled down and Liz bent to kiss her. 'Daddy says I can have a puppy for my own and he can sleep in my bedroom in his own bed and I can give him a name.'

It was the first night since Flyer had gone that she slept without waking and screaming in fear.

Four

The traffic on the motorway was stationary. Lou Barton rested her head against the steering wheel and groaned. She had been stuck in this queue for an hour now and it was the last thing she needed. Outside it was pitch-black except for the double string of red tail lights stretching far in front of her. Rain drummed on the roof and gusts of wind shook the small car. She had turned the engine off and the inside of the car was cold. She wanted to die.

The Memorial Service had been even worse than she had anticipated. She wished that Johnny's mother hadn't arranged it, that she hadn't gone. But how could she not go to her own husband's Memorial Service? A Memorial Service, instead of the funeral that had never happened. A Memorial Service to commemorate what would have been his birthday. He would have been thirty-two.

She could hear Johnny's voice saying,

'Hindsight is a wonderful thing'. He had always moved on from his mistakes, whereas she would agonize over hers for weeks. But he hadn't had the chance to say it this time. If only he hadn't been sent to New York that week, if only ... but Johnny had been so excited. 'It means more money, a promotion. They're trusting me with the possibility of a new contract, Lou! I can't believe it!'

So many plans: plans to renovate the cottage more quickly, a holiday, the baby they both longed for. Money in the bank and everything they had dreamed of together. Now the 'together' was gone and the dreams blown up along with Johnny.

No Johnny bursting into the house with a bunch of dandelions, a single red rose, a ridiculous brooch in the shape of a monkey.

No Johnny coming home at night with a smile on his face and a kiss for her lips, bursting into the house like a cyclone and hugging her until she begged for mercy.

How the memories hurt.

Imprisoned in the car, she had turned off the radio an hour ago. There was nothing she wanted to listen to. No music she liked, and only the empty promises of politicians that made her want to scream. Suddenly she remembered the *Just William* books. Her father had loved them when he was a boy and introduced them to her. It was Violet Elizabeth who threatened to 'thcream' until she was 'thick'! The memory made her smile and she wished she was less inhibited. How wonderful it would be to get out of the car in all the wind and rain and just do it! She knew she wouldn't but at least the thought made her feel a little better.

It was two years and nine days since she had first heard the news of the attack, and one month from that when she had finally given up hope.

How could she forget?

When every day was a day that she had to learn to live with it; every day was defined by trying to forget and failing.

The worst of it had been the loneliness, and her sense of isolation. She sometimes thought that it might have been easier if she'd lived in New York, where everybody was dealing with their loss together, and where everybody had known someone who had gone to work on that day and never come back. Here people tried to understand, but she and Johnny had been sufficient unto themselves. She had no family and his family...

That was what had been so dreadful about

today. Not the resurrection of grief, because grief had not faded, but the stark reality of her position in Johnny's family. Only Andrew, the vicar who had married them, and Johnny's brother had had a kind word for her, and a conciliatory squeeze on her arm when Johnny's aunt had made some tactless remark that perpetuated the family myth about Lou's place in Johnny's life. They had taken her into the kitchen and sat her down with a drink.

Andrew had sat down beside her and said, 'This must be horrible for you.'

Lou had tried to smile. 'It is. It's worse than I imagined. But how could I not come?'

He'd leaned back in his chair and asked, 'Is it getting any easier?'

She had shrugged and sighed. 'To be honest, I don't know. I manage to do what I have to do, but underneath it's as raw as yesterday. I can't believe it will ever heal. I try to think of other things, but it feels like a mortal wound.' She had looked at him and said, 'You ought to have some answers, Andrew. What do you say to people like me?'

'I don't always know what to say, Lou. I hate the platitudes of bereavement – time heals all; the dead are only in another room

– I can only speak to you from experience. I know that other people have said what you say, but life has moved them on into a place where they are in another room too. Not a room where their loved one still is, not a room where all they can feel is the stark reality of their loss, but a room where the view is different, better. You have to just let life take you there.'

Lou had smiled at him. 'Thank you for not pretending. I will try to remember. Even if I feel like I am stuck for ever, there's a train approaching that will take me away!'

He had laughed, hugged her and planted a kiss firmly on her cheek. 'There's your ticket for when it pulls up at the platform. I'll be thinking of you.'

It had been the only redeeming feature of the day. Lou supposed she was glad she had gone, just to hear that. She pressed her hand to her cheek. It was comforting to think of that ticket he had given her for no reason except love.

She was roused from her thoughts by a hoot from the car behind. The car in front of her had finally moved and those behind were getting impatient. She switched the ignition on and moved slowly forwards, the wipers sweeping through the deluge of rain still falling on to the windscreen. Her hopes rose as she actually changed into third gear; the end of the journey was suddenly a real possibility. But it was short-lived and, once again, the line of traffic became stationary.

She was so tired, bone-tired, and cold. She didn't want to run the engine whilst she wasn't moving and the interior of the car, chilled by the rain and wind outside, was less than comfortable. She yawned, huddled into her coat and closed her eyes.

This time her thoughts took her back to the first Christmas without Johnny. Well-meaning friends had invited her for the holiday and she had tried, really tried, for the sake of her hosts. But, inside, she had been a desert, and the loneliness had been unbearable.

Last year she had lied to everybody, and told her would-be hosts that she had already been invited elsewhere. All her presents were open before Christmas day; what was the point of waiting? She had eaten a fish finger sandwich for lunch and thought about clearing out the rest of Johnny's belongings.

The purple-and-yellow spotted tie given by his great aunt on their first Christmas together had undone her. She remembered so clearly his face when he had unwrapped it and draped it around his neck, solemnly reciting, '...and hideous tie, so kindly meant...' She had laughed and asked, 'Who wrote that then?'

'John Betjeman, my favourite poet,' he had replied.

A book of his poetry had appeared on her pillow one night and they had made a point of going to the places he had written about – sitting and reading a poem on the beach or train, a room in a cheap hotel, or on a cliff top with waves crashing on the rocks below. His poems were a diary for their life together.

She had buried the book at the back of her underwear drawer and the discovery of the tie had prompted her to get it out. Sitting on the floor, she had started to read. So many words, so many thoughts, so many memories, so many pictures, until at last she read, 'I love you, oh my darling, and what I can't make out is why since you have left me I'm somehow still about.'

They had laughed about it together once but it was those lines that had finally brought it home to her. She was and he wasn't. The rest of the day was a blank.

Another angry hoot roused her and once

again she started the engine. At last the long line of traffic kept moving and she finally reached the junction she needed to escape the motorway and start the next leg of her journey. Tiredness overwhelmed her again and she opened the window to try and rouse herself into some semblance of alertness. But the rain quickly soaked her and she had to close it. Her eyelids kept drooping and she was terrified she was going to fall asleep.

It was no good. She would have to stop.

The blue of a parking sign told her there would be a lay-by in one mile and she finally pulled into it with relief. It felt as if she was never going to get home. The car clock told her it was one o'clock in the morning. No wonder she was weary! The car heater wasn't warming her chilled bones; it was only making her sleepy.

Still the wind hammered at the car and the rain thundered on the roof. It seemed as if it would never stop. She wound the seat back to a reclining position and closed her eyes. Sleep claimed her.

She was woken by a tapping on the window. Adrenalin surged as she remembered gruesome urban myths she had heard about lonely travellers and axe murderers, but she was reassured to see the blue flashing light of a police car. She wound the window down and looked into the faces of two policemen. Their eyes were kindly, reassuring and, in the light of a torch one of them was holding, she could see the warrant cards in their hands.

'Are you all right? We were worried about you. It's late to be out here.'

'I'm fine. Just very tired. It's been a long day and there was a huge queue on the motorway. I should have been home hours ago, and I can't keep my eyes open.'

The policemen grinned, with rueful sympathy in their smiles. 'It's horrible, isn't it, when you get like that? A lorry jackknifed earlier on today and that's why the motorway was so awful. Have you got any coffee with you?'

'I wish I had!'

'There's an all-night transport café just up the road, about two miles on. Do you think you can make it that far?'

Lou looked at him, suddenly remembering. She and Johnny had stopped there once after a trip to his family. There would be bacon sandwiches, huge mugs of coffee, bread and butter, and ketchup in plastic tomatoes on the table. It suddenly sounded very attractive and she realized how hungry she was. Unable to eat during the day, and too churned up afterwards, she had hardly had anything since the early morning start and now, she realized, she could eat a horse!

'We'll escort you if you like. Make sure you get there safely. We usually stop there around now, anyway.'

'Thank you,' said Lou.

They drove at a sedate forty miles an hour and ten minutes later were pulling up in the car park of the café, its red, neon light a blur in the rain. They parked and Lou got out, moving stiffly at first after all those hours of sitting. She made a dash for the door of the café and one of the policemen pushed it open. Light spilled out along with the chatter of voices, the sound of music and the smell of coffee, bacon and sausages.

Inside, tables were pushed against the walls, their surfaces covered with plastic tablecloths brilliant with strawberries. The younger policeman pulled out a chair for her and invited her to sit. She smiled at him, and noticed how big he was. He towered above her, with dark hair curling at his neck, brown eyes in a sunburnt face, and a smile on his lips. 'I'll get you some coffee and you decide what you want to eat.'

Moments later he was back, holding the

most enormous mug of black coffee she had ever seen. He put it down in front of her and passed her the sugar bowl. 'Get yourself outside that and then have another one.'

A woman waved at him from behind the counter. She was comfortably large; her curves were swathed in an enormous green apron, she had hoop earrings dangling from her ears and her bright-red hair was piled on top of her head and skewered in place with an enormous tortoise shell hair slide. 'Who have you got there then? Are you arresting her?'

Lou's two companions laughed and explained, 'No, she was falling asleep so we rescued her and brought her into your tender care, Meg!'

Meg reached behind the counter and handed the policemen two packages and two lidded plastic cups of coffee. 'Here're your provisions for the night, you two. Off you go and do some work for a change.'

They laughed at her mockery and said, 'All right, all right, we're going!'

The younger one grinned at Lou and put his thumb up. 'Meg will look after you. She's an expert, she is.'

Meg looked at Lou and she felt as if the woman noticed everything there was to be noticed. She felt as if she had been read like a book.

'You've come to the right place, duck. We'll feed you up, wake you up, settle you down and see you safely on your way, never fear!'

Five

For a moment Lou felt lost – alone in this place in the middle of the night. The other customers stared at her but Meg snapped at them, 'Come on, you lot. She'll have to charge you for looking if you don't get back to your own business,' and then sat down opposite Lou. 'It's nice to have some female company,' she said. 'There aren't many who come in here.'

'Don't you get frightened by yourself? It seems so isolated.'

Meg laughed. 'Maybe I would if I was by myself, but I have a friend.' She whistled and from behind the counter padded a large Rottweiler.

Lou gasped, intimidated by the size of the animal.

'Come on, my beauty,' said Meg and he loped over and rested his head on her knee. Meg scratched between his ears and he closed his eyes in ecstasy. Meg laughed. 'He's a pussycat really. One of the dog handlers trained him for me, in return for free food. If there's trouble he soon gets it sorted out. So no, I don't worry about being out here by myself.' She patted the dog. 'Not with you around, eh?' she said to him.

Then Meg looked up at Lou and said briskly, 'Now, what are you going to have to eat? You look absolutely exhausted. Like a waif or stray.'

The unexpected kindness, after the awfulness of the day, took Lou unawares. Tears welled and she scrabbled in her pocket for a tissue.

Meg looked at her for a moment and said, 'I'll go and cook you the Full English, and then come and sit with you while you eat. The loo's over there if you want to freshen up.' She pointed at a door at the end of the building and Lou smiled, grateful for the woman's consideration.

'Thanks,' Lou said. 'Full English will be lovely. I'm glad you decided for me!' She headed to the safety of the Ladies with relief. Away from the curious eyes of the other customers she had time to recover herself. She splashed her face with cold water and dried it on a paper towel, tried to bring some order to her dishevelled hair and attempted to put a smile on her face. She would be glad of Meg's company.

When she returned, Meg was just depositing a large tray on the table. She placed a plate in front of Lou. There was bacon – lean and perfectly cooked – fat, brown sausages, a slice of black pudding, two fried eggs, several halves of fried tomato, a gigantic mushroom, a slice of fried bread and a rack full of toast. Another large mug of coffee joined it and Meg finally placed a cup of tea on the table for herself.

'Come on, lass. Eat up. You'll feel better after that lot!'

Lou wondered if she would ever finish it but once she had started eating she quickly cleared the plate.

Meg laughed at her as she mopped up the last of the juices with a piece of toast. 'You were hungry, weren't you?' She hesitated for a moment, then said, 'You don't have to tell me if you don't want to but you look like it might do you good to talk. You've obviously had an awful day.'

Her matter-of-fact manner appealed to

Lou. It reminded her of the vicar and his lack of sanctimonious offerings. His words came back to her and she laughed.

Meg looked at her and said, 'What's the joke?'

Lou said, 'I suddenly wondered if you are a train!'

'Well, I've been called a few things in my life, but never that.' She chuckled and asked, 'Why a train?'

Lou found herself explaining. Somehow, it was easy to talk to Meg. She seemed like someone for whom life held no surprises. 'I've been to my husband's Memorial Service. He died in the 9/11 terrorist attacks two years ago. I didn't want to go but I felt I had to. His mother arranged it. It was horrible. That's what the vicar said to me. That I had to let life take me somewhere else – into another room. I said I'd try to remember, if I felt I was going nowhere, that there was a train approaching just waiting for me to climb aboard.'

She sighed and drank some coffee. 'I can't talk about it to anybody. Everybody is embarrassed – caught up in their own inability to deal with it. They all skirt round the subject and I end up protecting them from my own truths.' She paused, and said, 'You seem like someone who knows what's what. It's nice to just talk about it without instant withdrawal. So maybe you are a train for me!'

Meg laughed and patted Lou's hand. 'Go on then. Tell me about him. What was his name?'

'Johnny. He was called Johnny. We'd only been married three years. We met in London in a thunderstorm, both trying to get in the door of a café at the same time. He bought me a huge Cappuccino and we talked for hours. In three months we were engaged and in six months we were married.'

'Wow!' said Meg. 'A whirlwind romance. It must have been love at first sight.'

Lou grinned, 'It was, nearly. We did have a few rough patches on the way though. I suppose that was part of the awfulness of today because they were always to do with his family. Especially his mother.'

'Why was that then?'

'She was the most controlling woman I have ever met. So unlike my own mother. Johnny used to say she should have been Managing Director of a multinational company; then she could have exhausted her ambitions on the workforce and her career instead of the family. She felt she had the right to decide who her children should marry and woe betide if you went against her wishes.' She laughed. 'Johnny used to say she had a doctorate in emotional blackmail.'

'So, I take it she didn't want you and Johnny to marry?'

'She certainly didn't! When she was in the maternity hospital having Johnny there was another woman there who she got very friendly with. She was "our sort", was what his mother said, and she had a baby girl born the day after Johnny. The two of them have been conniving ever since for a marriage between their babies. They put this disgusting expression on their faces and say, "It was meant to be".'

Meg laughed. 'I can just picture it. What did Johnny think about it?'

'Oh, he loathed her! Her name was Mabel and she changed it to Maybelline when she was fourteen. That's what comes of being brought up as the heroine of a fairy tale. Johnny used to call her "The Haunt" because she was always there at every event, following him around. He and his brother used to play tricks on her so Johnny could escape.'

'And what happened when you appeared?'

'I'm cast as "The Scarlet Woman from London" who lured Johnny away from his one true love and cast a spell on him.'

'I suppose Maybelline was there today?'

'Was she! Dressed in black and wearing a hat with a little veil, pretending *she* was the widow and not me! It made me feel so angry. The terrorists destroyed Johnny but it feels as if she is stealing the rest of my reality. As though my marriage with Johnny never happened and I have no right to my grief.'

'Of course you do. What would your husband have said to you?'

Lou grimaced. 'He'd have told me not to go. Then, when I said that I wished I hadn't, he would have said, "Hindsight is a wonderful thing". Then he would have said, "Don't let them get to you," and then he would have said, "Grab life with both hands. You only have it once."' Her face crumpled and once again her eyes filled with tears. 'I don't seem to be doing a very good job of it.'

Meg said nothing for a moment. Her thoughts were elsewhere, travelling her own journey. Remembering how *she* had felt. She reached across and put her hand over Lou's where they rested on the tablecloth. She was twisting her wedding band, which was loose on her ring finger. 'The worst of it is coming to terms with all the might-have-beens,' Meg said.

Lou sighed. 'Yes. The cottage that would be perfectly restored. The children we would have had together; our own family. All the happy memories; all the dreams come true. It's thoughts of the children we'd planned for that are the hardest. Everything had changed for the better when he got the promotion that took him to New York. We were going to start a family, and could afford to get a lot of work done on the cottage instead of doing it bit by bit. Now, when I see children I feel like a bitter and twisted woman. I can't bear to be around them: not my niece who was at the service and not the baby that my neighbours have. And it's such hard work, trying to not have those feelings.'

'Where are you living?'

'Still in the cottage. It's called Brookside. It was paradise for us. Down a narrow winding lane, in the middle of nowhere, with only a few neighbours. Lots of space for children to play, and peace and quiet for us. All I can see is trees and fields and sky and the stream where a heron comes and swans nest. We both loved it, but it's a lonely spot to be by yourself. I don't want to move because at least I do have *memories* of Johnny in that place of the life we had together. I feel as though Maybelline will have won if I move. So I'm not going to.'

'That sounds very sensible,' said Meg, 'and it sounds like what your Johnny would have said to you too. Go for it, girl!' She got up and started loading the debris from the meal on to the tray, and then disappeared into the kitchen behind the counter.

The door slammed open and a young man burst in. He had bright-green spiky hair, and wore tight jeans and a T-shirt that said 'I'm a Killer' on it. Pausing on the threshold he looked around and smirked. He swaggered over to Lou, saying, 'Hello, darling, it must be my lucky night.'

As he came closer she could smell beer on his breath, and she eyed him warily. He moved round behind her and put his hands on her shoulders, lifting one to stroke her hair. She shuddered and he mocked, 'Exciting you, am I? Can't wait to go outside with me? Come on then, darling.' His hand grasped her by the arm and he tried to pull her to her feet.

Lou grabbed hold of the edge of the table

and screamed out, 'Meg! Meg!'

The two remaining customers jumped to their feet and moved towards the man saying loudly, 'Leave the lady alone and get out.'

The young man eyed them up and sneered, 'Yeah, and who's going to make me? Not you two, that's for sure.'

Meg's deep voice sounded from the counter. 'Not them, maybe, but Venn will. Get him, boy. Go on.'

The young man turned and snarled, 'There's nobody can stop me.' He pulled at Lou again. 'Come on, darling. We can go for a ride together.' He leered at her. 'You won't regret it.'

Lou felt sick. She was terrified by the unexpectedness of him, his unpredictability, his strength and his drunkenness. Then she heard a low growl followed by a whistle. Venn bounded across the room and seized the young man's wrist in his huge jaws.

The man paled and shouted, 'Get him off, get him off!' He tried to wrench his arm from Venn's jaws, but the dog gripped him even harder. A low growl rumbled again in his throat. 'I could sue you for this,' the man shouted. His words were slurred.

Meg laughed. 'Ha! He hasn't hurt you yet,

and there are plenty of people here who can describe your behaviour towards this lady. No, your *attack* on this lady. Now get out and don't come back. Ever.' She looked at the dog and pointed, commanding, 'Take him out, Venn.'

The dog kept a firm hold of his wrist and walked towards the door. The young man disappeared, shouting obscenities.

Lou collapsed at the table and Meg came up to her. 'I'm so sorry. Just what you don't need. We don't usually have his sort in here.'

The other two customers called Meg over and they had a hurried conversation. She came back and said, 'They've suggested I call the police and they can escort you home, make sure you're safe. I'll report it too. He's a menace that one. And he's drunk. Now, what do you think?'

Lou nodded. She had started to tremble from the shock of the encounter, and wasn't even sure that she was safe to drive herself. The thought of that horrible man lying in wait for her was terrifying. What if he followed her to the cottage? The worst could happen. She had felt lonely there, but never afraid.

It seemed an age before the police arrived. Lou recognized them as her saviours from the lay-by and was pleased to see them. They came up to her, full of concern. 'What a thing to happen. Are you OK?'

Lou looked up at them. 'I am, but I'm not sure I'm fit to drive. I'm afraid I feel rather weak at the knees.'

'I'm not surprised.' It was the older man who spoke. 'Why don't you let Ray drive your car? I'll follow in the police car.'

Ray said, 'We've had trouble with him before, but we saw his car heading the opposite direction to yours. We've got a car out after him, too, so he won't get away with it. Don's suggestion sounds like a good idea. OK with you?'

Lou grimaced. 'I don't want to do anything about his behaviour. Please.'

'Don't worry, you won't need to. He's certainly over the limit. We'll see you home though, just to make sure. And we'll sort him out too.'

'Thank you,' said Lou. 'You really have been my guardian angels tonight!' She smiled at Meg. 'And you! Thank you for listening.'

'You take good care of her! And come back again, Lou. Let me know where the train is taking you!'

'I will!' shouted Lou as she headed out the

door. At last, she was going home. The thought of the empty house daunted her. Perhaps Don and Ray would come in for a drink. She could not imagine sleeping that night. The coffee had been strong and that, combined with fright, had left her wide awake. Would the day never end?

Six

Flyer fought – twisting and trying to escape from the piercing grasp of the claws in his back. The buzzard flew on but Flyer was strong and agile; once the initial shock had faded he had no intention of surrendering to his foe. He struggled and, twisting in the air, struck at his attacker's belly, scratching and biting. The hungry buzzard dropped lower, his talons still firmly anchored, but he was young and inexperienced and had not expected his quarry to fight back.

Beneath them the world had changed into a speeding blur as cars, people, fields and houses flashed by. Fear lent Flyer strength and he gave an immense thrust with his back legs, driving his claws, again and again, up and into the soft belly of the bird. It made the talons twist deep into his shoulder but his terror and his need to escape made him oblivious to his own pain. The buzzard, feeling knives in his belly, finally gave up the battle and opened his talons.

Flyer, more dead than alive, tumbled earthwards. He landed heavily on a grass embankment and rolled under a bush. The fall drove the breath from his body and he lay almost senseless. Consciousness slowly returned and this time he did not dare move a muscle. He remembered the lessons he had learned and then forgotten:

Do not move when danger threatens.

Above him the angry bird, frustrated of his prey, hovered. Flyer lay still, hidden under the bush. He could sense the bird – still waiting, still hoping – but he would not give him another chance.

He had never felt such pain. Every bone, every muscle, every fibre of his being ached and there was a fiercely sharp throb in his shoulders where the talons had torn skin and muscle, and his own struggles had worsened the wounds. He mewed forlornly, trying to move, but excruciating pain seared in his hindquarters. The buzzard sensed the tiny movement and flew up again, but a lorry thundering past created a draft, which blew the bird off course. Flyer lay still – afraid to move in case it brought back the pain.

Frustrated, and unable to see the kitten any more, the buzzard flew away to look for something smaller – something that would not fight back with such aggression.

Flyer rested; he was both exhausted and terrified. Slowly, the different smells and noises of the place he had fallen into came to him and his fear intensified. Cars and lorries thundered past, throwing up clouds of spray. There was a horrible smell and those deafening noises that faded and grew louder, faded and grew louder.

It had started to rain hard and, even under the bush, the rain got through, plastering his fur to his body and spreading the blood on his shoulders into a red stain through his lighter fur. It seemed as though the world was full of monsters – roaring dragons determined to hunt him down and devour him. He lay still and waited, although for what he did not know. Only wanting rest and safety – the warmth of a lap, people and voices to comfort him, hands to soothe, someone to talk to.

Hunger pangs stirred in his belly and he

knew he needed to find food. Instinct and the need to survive was strong in him – as strong as the lure of the scents had been earlier, which had teased him and tantalized him away from the safety of the farm. The survival instinct finally drove him out from shelter. It was easier to go down than up and he dragged himself slowly, inch by painful inch, resting frequently. He knew the farm lay on the other side of this place where the dragons thundered past and he struggled to cross it.

Darkness came and the volume of traffic dropped. He reached the central reservation and lay there, almost unconscious, growing colder by the minute. Again the will to survive drove him on and he slowly inched across the other carriageway – one or two cars passing and not noticing the sodden little body that, miraculously, their wheels swept past.

At last he reached the other side and stopped again. There was almost no strength left in him, but faintly he could smell blood. A young rabbit had been killed and the scent of its flesh roused Flyer to one last effort. He moved towards it at a slow, desperate crawl and then stopped – terror grabbing him again as an approaching car almost hit him, but braked and came to a halt. Another car pulled up behind, lights flashing. Then people bent over him. He mewed, producing only a faint squeak.

Lou stared down at the injured kitten. There were no houses for miles around. How on earth had it got there? She bent down to him and he mewed again. The faint noise was barely audible.

'He must have been hit by a car and been here for hours. He's absolutely soaked and bleeding, poor little beast.'

Flyer gazed up at her, his agony reflected in his pleading eyes. The lady knelt on the wet road and he mewed again, pain overwhelming him, as she picked him up and cradled him.

'You're right,' said the younger policeman. 'He must have been run over. He's in a terrible state.'

Lou hated to see an animal in pain. 'We can't just leave him here to die.' She felt so *angry*. 'Someone must have dumped him and hoped he would be killed. I'm not going to let it happen. I'll take him home. If he does die in the night, at least he won't die alone. And if he survives we can find him a vet.'

Flyer mewed again, and Lou gazed at him,

her face anxious. 'I think he's agreeing with me.' She touched his head gently and said, 'There's life in you yet, isn't there?'

Flyer felt comforted. It might not be Zannie or Liz, but there was kindness in the voice.

Dawn was a breath away and the traffic building again. The rain had at last stopped and cars slowed, curious about the story behind the scene at the edge of the dual carriageway. 'You could phone the PDSA first thing,' said one of the policemen. 'They would take care of him.'

For the first time in a long while Lou felt the stirring of a need: something she really wanted, something she wanted to fight for. She felt the smallest throb of a purr in the body she cradled and she knew she was going to fight for him. She walked back to her car and the younger policeman opened the door for her. 'There's a rug on the back seat. I'll put it on my lap and wrap him in it while you drive,' she said.

Flyer lay quietly. He didn't like the car, its strange smell or the noise of the engine, but he trusted the lady carrying him; he knew she was going to care for him.

Lou looked at Ray and said, 'It's a good job you were driving. I don't think I'd have noticed him if I had been. I can't thank you enough for your kindness.'

'We'll see you home, just to make sure you get there safely. It's been a hell of a day and a night for you. I don't think either of us will rest easy until we know you're back safely. We're off duty now too.'

Ray was getting over the desertion of his girlfriend and Lou was attractive, despite her exhausted appearance. Her hair, blonde and thick, fell smoothly to her shoulders and swept away from her forehead to reveal finely-arched eyebrows and eyes of a clear blue-grey. Her face looked drawn with fatigue and there were dark shadows under her eyes. He wondered what she would be like if she really smiled or laughed. A stunner, he suspected. She had the same air of vulnerability as the rescued kitten at the moment.

Lou smiled at him and said thank you. She was glad of their company. Perhaps they would both come in and have a hot drink before going home. The day would end differently to the way it had started – with company in the house and this scrap of life, which was gazing up at her with blue, pain-filled eyes. Desperately, she willed him to live.

Seven

It was still several miles to Lou's house. The little cat made faint noises as he struggled to find a comfortable position. He lay still – lost with the change in his world, and not understanding – his senses overwhelmed by the strangeness of it all. His body ached with pain and his heart ached for familiarity. His life had become a nightmare. In the end, all he could hang on to was trust in this person he was with.

Ray signalled left and turned off down the slip road. He drove carefully, anxious not to cause the kitten additional pain. One final right-hand turn by the old church and they were on the narrow, unsurfaced lane that led down to Brookside. The blackness of the night enveloped them. Ray inched forward. He was acutely aware of the ruts and pot-holes, which were a deterrent for visitors sometimes. Stone walls banked with grass loomed on either side and he was worried he might scrape the car.

The kitten mewed and Lou stroked him gently under the rug to calm him. 'Hang in there, nearly home,' she said to him.

'It *is* lonely down here,' said Ray. 'Are you the only house?'

'No, not quite,' said Lou. 'There's a derelict farmhouse right at the end. In-between there's a place called Twisted Willows Cottage where a man called Jeff lives, and another called The Bramble Patch where a woman called Janet lives. We pass each other on the lane sometimes and wave, but that's all.'

Their names had been enough. She and Johnny had had each other.

Ray pulled into the driveway of her house and parked up.

Lou said, 'The front-door key is the one hanging from the leather tag. Why don't you unlock the door and let us in?'

The rain had stopped at last. Lou got out, holding the kitten carefully, as Don climbed out of the police car that had followed them in. A gust of wind caught his door and slammed it shut. A moment later a light glimmered through the hedge and Lou said ruefully, 'Oh dear, I think we've woken my neighbour.'

Don and Ray followed Lou inside and into

the hall. Doors led off on either side of the hall and she went through one into the kitchen, with the policemen following behind. It had an unused look. There was no clutter of pans and dishes – the paraphernalia of someone who enjoyed cooking and eating there. Lou looked round, grimaced, and said to them, 'Why don't you go through to the living room?'

She handed Ray the kitten and said, 'You hold him for a minute while I find something to dry him off and make him more comfortable. Would you both like a drink?'

They nodded and Don said, 'But get the kitten sorted first. We can wait.'

She showed them through and they sat down. Here, too, there was no clutter of family life – no discarded shoes and clothes, books and magazines, half-empty coffee cups – nothing that anybody had felt like dropping as they rushed through the business of their life. It felt as though the house was holding its breath.

Suddenly, Ray found himself hoping, as hard as Lou obviously did, that this little scrap of fur they had rescued would still have life in it tomorrow. He noticed a framed photograph on the mantelpiece: a tall man wearing a blue fleece jacket, laughing at the camera. He was clean-shaven, his straight, blond hair blowing on a wind that frothed the sea behind into white-capped waves, and he was making a ‘thumbs up’ sign at the photographer. Beside the photograph was a pile of shells topped with a dried-out strand of seaweed. It looked like a memorial to something and he realized they still didn’t know how Lou had spent her day; what mission had brought her to this particular ending. What was certain was that the man in the photograph was no longer on the scene.

In the kitchen, Lou switched on the kettle and took three mugs off the hooks under the saucepan shelf. At least the house was warmed by the central heating. It would have been too horrible to have come back to a cold house.

Flyer stared round at unfamiliar walls and furniture. Where was the smell of the farmhouse? Of the other animals? Of the kitchen, which was always filled with the scent of baking and other tantalizing smells that made him want to find out what they were and taste the source? He felt lost, exhausted by pain and numbed with cold.

Lou tipped hot water from the kettle into a small bowl and added cold water. She dipped a finger to make sure it wasn't too hot and opened a drawer to dig out some cotton wool. There was a cardboard box in the utility room and she cut the front down halfway and lined it with an old towel pulled from a cupboard. After thinking for a moment she dashed upstairs to fetch a hot-water bottle and filled it with hot water from the kettle and cold from the tap. It would be terrible to burn the little fellow but he needed to be warmed. She wrapped the bottle in another towel and placed it in the box.

In the living room she knelt beside Ray. The kitten looked as if he was barely breathing. Carefully, she bathed the angry wounds in his neck, and then patted his fur dry with wads of kitchen towel. He lay patiently on Ray's lap, allowing her to tend him. She gently lifted him and laid him in the box against the warmth of the hot-water bottle, covering him with the edge of the towel so that just his face peeped out. He looked up at her, his eyes barely open, and tried to mew. No more than a squeak emerged.

They looked down at the pathetic little scrap and Lou said, 'I wonder if he'll drink something?'

A minute later she was back with a bowl of warmed milk. She squatted beside the box and placed a drop on his mouth. He opened it and a little, pink tongue caught the milk and licked at it. Lou picked up a teaspoon and carefully held it for him. He tried to drink and, between them, a few spoonfuls disappeared. It was a start.

'That's a good sign,' said Lou. 'Now it's our turn to have a drink.'

'I don't know about you,' said Don, 'but I think I'm more ready for my bed.'

Ray nodded and said, 'We'll be on our way. I'm sure you'll need to sleep.'

Lou yawned. 'In theory I suppose I do. But I've drunk so much coffee and I'm so wired up with all that has happened that I don't think I shall be able to. It's only an hour or two before I can expect to get hold of a vet. No, I think I'll stay up and keep this little fellow company. I'll look in the yellow pages for a vet.'

'You don't need to do that,' said Ray. 'You need Jake Commers. He's the one we have for the police dogs and I know he's good. If anyone can sort this beastie out he can. I'll give him a call for you and warn him.' He laughed and said ruefully, 'Our black Labrador "Scop" is a regular patient of his. He's always up to some mischief. Last week he ate a cake of soap.'

Lou gasped. 'What? A whole bar! Wasn't he sick?'

'He was in the end, but Jake pointed out that he had very clean insides! I reckon he's on the way to buying Jake a Mercedes. His escapades cost me a fortune.' Ray tore the top sheet off a handy notepad and drew a quick map for her.

'Oh, I know where that is,' she said. 'I've driven past it often enough on my way to Larksbridge. I never thought I might need to use him though.'

Ray and Don left and Lou bolted the door after them. She went back to the living room and put the box down on the floor beside her favourite chair. Johnny used to laugh at her, saying she was like a little dormouse, the way she curled up in it. She did so now – wrapping herself in a rug from the settee and looking down on the little animal. His eyes were closed and he lay completely still. Dread filled her and she touched his head with one finger. To her relief he opened his eyes and tried to lift his head. 'Oh, thank goodness,' she whispered to him. 'You must not die on me. You mustn't give up. Keep fighting, little one. We can do it together.' In spite of the coffee she soon found her eyes closing and she dozed off.

Flyer did not like being alone. He needed comfort and he intended to get it. The warmth and the milk had revived him a little and, when he tried, he managed to stand on his front legs and struggle to the edge of the box. Then he stretched for the side of the chair and began to inch, slowly and painfully, up the side. His rear end refused to do what he wanted but he was determined.

Lou was woken by a scratching sound and a faint, demanding mew. She opened her eyes and gazed in astonishment as the kitten crawled over the arm of her chair and flopped into her lap. 'Well, you are a fighter!' she said.

Flyer tried to settle himself comfortably, cuddled against her. Pain still dominated but at least he now had the warmth of a human close to him.

The kitten licked her hand, the roughness of his tongue surprising Lou. It made her laugh, as she imagined Johnny saying, 'Twenty-six and never been licked by a cat!'

The kitten settled and slept and, soon, sleep claimed Lou. His warmth was a comfort for her too.

Lou was awoken by the ring of the doorbell. She put the still-sleeping kitten back in his box and staggered to her feet, stiff from sleeping in the chair. Who could be calling at this time? It was only eight o'clock. She opened the door to find Ray standing there.

'Good morning,' he said. He looked at her as she rubbed her eyes. 'I see you did manage to get some sleep then. How is your guest?'

Lou grinned. 'He's still alive! He's a real fighter. You wouldn't believe it. He managed to get himself out of the box and up on to my lap. We both slept in the chair.'

Pleased at the good news, Ray grinned back at her. 'That's great. Jake's expecting you. I thought the little fellow could do with some attention as soon as possible so I called him. He can meet you at the surgery in half an hour.'

Lou looked at her watch, still feeling half-asleep. She felt bedraggled and uncomfortable, and realized she hadn't even changed out of the clothes she had worn yesterday.

'You go on and get washed and changed if you want. I can sit with the kitten for a few minutes and I'll take you to meet Jake. You can hold him on your lap then and he'll feel safer.'

'OK. Thank you. Could you try him with some more milk?'

'I will and I'll make a coffee ready for you when you come down.'

Lou hurried upstairs. There was time to have a quick shower, drag a brush through her hair and change her clothes. Once downstairs she gulped down the coffee and asked, 'Did he have any milk?'

'No, not this time. But perhaps it's a good job if he's going to need an anaesthetic.'

Lou looked at the kitten. In the cold light of day he looked worse than he had before. His wounds had bled again and he looked almost lifeless. It seemed cruel to even try to move him but she knew that the trip to the vet was his only hope. She lifted the box and they walked out to the car. She was glad it was no longer the police car – especially when they passed the postman on the way up the lane.

They were soon at the vet's and he greeted them at the door. He glanced briefly at Lou, and then peered into the box she carried. 'Poor little scrap,' he said. 'You should have rung me earlier. I'm on call twenty-four hours, you know.'

Ray interrupted, 'I did call you, Jake, but you were out on a calving. And this young lady hadn't exactly had an easy day herself.'

Jake grunted and said, 'Sorry. I just don't

like to think of him suffering any longer than he has to.'

Lou glared at him and snapped back, 'No, nor do I.'

'OK, OK, he's here now. Bring him inside and let's have a look at him.'

Jake lifted the little cat carefully out of the box and put him on the examination table. He parted the fur on his neck with gentle fingers and examined the wounds. 'It wasn't a road accident. He's been taken by a bird ... a buzzard, an owl or maybe a peregrine. It looks as if he fought back and got himself dropped.'

'I'm glad he wasn't just dumped,' said Lou. 'Has he broken his back legs?'

Jake continued to examine the animal, his fingers moving gently, looking for injuries. 'I'm not sure. There's certainly something the matter back there. I'd have to X-ray to see what's going on.'

Lou gulped and asked, 'What do you think his chances are of surviving?' She felt frightened, and expected that she looked it too.

'Probably fifty-fifty. If you found him last night I'd guess he had been out in that awful weather for a while. He'll be suffering from shock and exposure as well.' He looked at her and said, 'He's going to need some very expensive treatment. It'll be difficult to trace his owners. Goodness knows how far he came before being dropped. He is very distinctive though, isn't he? Siamese, without a doubt.'

He stroked the kitten's soft fur and said, 'He's well looked after and was healthy before this. What do you want me to do? Putting him to sleep is the kindest thing to do, considering his condition.'

'No!' shouted Lou, and then put her hand to her mouth in embarrassment. 'I'm sorry, but I just couldn't bear to have him put down yet. Not after he managed to climb on to my lap last night.' She looked at Jake and said, 'I'll pay, whatever it costs. We'll advertise that we've found him and I'll look after him. I know he's a fighter. He didn't go through all that battle to escape the bird and be found by me just to be put quietly to sleep.'

Jake nodded. 'Right then, we'll see what we can do. The wounds in his shoulder need cleaning and stitching. I'll need to take X-rays. He'll need antibiotics and we'll have to put him on a drip for a few days whilst he's recovering.'

'It sounds a lot, but I still want him to have the chance.'

Jake didn't say anything. He didn't feel he could refuse, but he was not optimistic. 'We'll have to keep him in for a week to ten days,' he said and continued, 'Have you ever owned a cat?' Lou shook her head and he called through to the nurse in reception. 'Alison? Could you fetch me one of the leaflets about cat care?'

It can't be that difficult, thought Lou. *Other people manage it. I'm sure I can.* She remembered the kitten's attempts last night and thought that, if he survived, she wouldn't need a book. If anything wasn't right he would soon tell her about it!

Suddenly, there was something to look forward to. She thought of a small, impatient animal greeting her with fervour when she came home. Of playing games with him. Of his comforting presence on her lap in the evenings, and maybe sleeping on her bed at night.

Another living creature in the house. If only he survived.

Eight

Janet Leigh stood at the sink in the kitchen of The Bramble Patch and gazed out of the window. It was a view she usually loved but today, her hands busy with washing the single bowl and mug she had used for breakfast, she longed for some sign of human life.

There was the heron, a grey sentinel, standing patient on the far bank of the stream that flowed at the bottom of her garden. Toffee-coloured cows grazed in the field on the other side and soft-furred brown rabbits nibbled in the hedge bottoms. A magpie flew up from one of the apple trees where the bird feeders hung and she said, 'Hello, Mr Magpie, you're looking very fine today!' They were the first words she had spoken out loud for nearly a week.

Breakfast had been a bowl of muesli – the last, dusty remnants from the packet – and an apple with puckering skin. She knew she needed to go out, brave the bus ride to town and the shelves of the supermarket, but it was so much effort and she dreaded the possibility of one of her anxiety attacks. Out there felt so dangerous.

All those strangers, busy with their own lives; in the shop loud music crashed and pounded out its rhythms, stopping her from thinking clearly. There were products on the top shelf that she couldn't reach and elusive assistants who were never there when she needed them. Then the struggle home with the bags on the bus and back down the lane to her house.

The alarm call of a blackbird roused her from her dreaming and she told herself sternly, 'Come on, Janet. Pull yourself together. You chose this, remember? Now get on with it!'

She could imagine her father saying 'the devil finds work for idle hands' to her. A lay preacher of the fire and brimstone variety, he had damned many of life's little pleasures. The list had seemed endless – pretty clothes, reading in bed, cinema, television, dancing, pop music, a glass of sherry, getting up later than seven o'clock in the morning. She envied her friends, who had been allowed to enjoy the pleasures of life and to believe that God had created the world for people to enjoy, instead of it being a trap made by the devil.

From the radio, she heard the last of the weather forecast – a depression, bringing strong winds and heavy rain by mid-afternoon, and persisting into the night. Clouds were indeed beginning to gather on the horizon; rearing mounds of grey and white obliterated the distant mountains. If she was going to go, she had better go now. She sighed and went to look for her handbag, coat and shoes.

Ten minutes later she was picking her way down the lane – avoiding the puddles that lay in the ruts and keeping to the central ridge of tufted grass. When she had first seen the cottage, the lane had delighted her. Used to the stark greys and blacks of the town roads, with the constant roar of traffic day and night, this had seemed a heaven on earth. It had seemed just what she wanted – to spend the legacy from her mother on this little house in the middle of nowhere.

Driving home from work it had always felt as if she left the troubles of the day at the lane end as she turned off the road and on to the rough track. All the bickering, the budget battles, the petty trivia of the working day could stay there for the night. Home was a haven of peace, and her pleasures the garden, the birds, and the pickings from the hedgerows with their rich, autumnal crops. Now though she felt as if some malign force was working on her. She couldn't say when or where it had come from. It would be easier to understand if there had been some climactic personal event to mark the change in her; then she would understand it better, be able to do something about it.

But it had crept up on her ... an enemy slowly invading every aspect of her life.

Lou, her neighbour, was out again. There was no car parked on the drive and the house had a neglected look. Weeds flourished in the front borders and Janet longed to wade in and pull them out.

But she hardly knew her.

She remembered when Lou and her husband had first moved in. The garden had been always full of their laughter and there had always been some project in progress. All that had changed though, and Janet had been shaken to the core when she'd heard the news of his death.

The bus trundled past the end of the lane. She knew it would wait for five minutes at the stop by the post office but she quickened her pace as much as her grumbling knee would let her. At the bungalow on the corner, the young woman was hanging her washing. Minute vests and all-in-one suits flapped on the line, and from the house came the demanding cries of a hungry baby.

The woman waved at Janet and called cheerfully, 'Hello there!' She grimaced. 'I've run out of clothes again! Three pairs of everything, they said. More like ten, I think!' She looked anxiously at the sky. 'I do hope the rain holds off until this lot is dry.'

Janet laughed. 'Me too. I certainly don't want to lug my shopping home in the rain!'

The exchange lifted her spirits and she smiled at the bus driver as she showed her bus pass and went to sit down. She thought of the washing line and those sweet little pink and white suits dancing in the wind. In her childhood it would have been a line of terry nappies flapping on the breeze – semaphore flags announcing 'baby lives here'.

Daydreaming, she was startled by the driver's sharp voice, saying, 'Are you getting off then?' Embarrassed and blushing furiously she rummaged for her bags and hurried down the bus. As she did so she heard him mutter, 'About time too.'

Her spirits plummeted and she felt like returning to her seat and just going home.

Again, she told herself, *Just do it, Janet. Don't be pathetic!* As she stepped off the bus the first heavy raindrops began to fall from a sky that was black with clouds. If only it had held off for another hour or two. Now she was going to get soaked.

At the supermarket she ticked the last item off her list and made her way to the checkout. Only one till manned and a long queue – trolleys piled high with the weekly shop for what looked like families with ten children.

How long was this going to take?

She didn't want to miss the bus and have to wait an hour for the next one. The familiar panic started and she struggled to calm herself.

Hurry up, hurry up, hurry up, she said in her head. To her relief, a young woman wearing the supermarket's uniform bustled up to another till and called to her, 'Would you like to come over to this one?'

A woman in a multicoloured coat dashed from the end of one aisle and made a beeline for the same till. The two trolleys collided and Janet stumbled. She glared at the queue-jumper, who gasped and put her hand over her mouth for a moment.

'Oh God, I've done it again,' the queue-jumper said. 'I am so sorry. I'm in such a rush to get back to my father that I'm not thinking straight. He gets really cross if I take longer than he thinks I should. Why don't you go first?' She adjusted her glasses, which had slipped down her nose, and stared at Janet. 'Well, I never!' she said. 'I know you! It's Janet, isn't it? From the library at Larksbridge?'

Janet stared back at her, remembering. It was the coat that reminded her. This was the woman who used to come in to borrow books and to tell stories to the children on a Saturday morning or in the school holidays. She smiled, remembering the sight of a group of children sitting wide-eyed and silent in front of her whilst she told them a Greek legend or a condensed version of one of Shakespeare's plays. She had been magical and Janet had used to wish she could abandon her duties and sit down too. The woman hadn't changed – still looking somewhere between a bag lady and a peasant from some rural tradition. Her long, black hair was still loosely knotted at the nape of her neck, beads still fought for space round her neck and she was wearing her habitual purple, fingerless gloves.

'It's Frances, isn't it?' Janet said. 'How

lovely to meet you again.'

The young woman at the till coughed noisily and stared at them both. Other shoppers were gathering behind them.

Frances said, 'Go on, you go first. Here, I'll unload while you pack.'

'Oh, thank you,' said Janet. 'That would be really helpful. I have a bus to catch in...' She paused and looked at her watch. 'Oh no. It'll be going in ten minutes...'

Frances started piling items on to the belt, asking, 'Where are you living now?'

'Out at Marshley,' replied Janet, fumbling for her purse and shopping bags in her capacious handbag. 'I moved there before I retired.'

'Well, I never,' said Frances, as she pulled tins out of the trolley. 'That's where my dad lives. Look, why don't you come back with me for a cuppa and I'll take you and your shopping home afterwards?'

'No,' protested Janet. 'I can't do that! What will your father think?'

'Oh, he's a darling really. Just a bit short tempered at times. He's a cat with sheathed claws. He might spit a bit but he never bites or scratches.' She laughed, not noticing Janet's expression at the mention of cats.

'Well, it would be nice. Go on then. Thank

you.'

Ten minutes later they were bowling along the road in a battered old Ford, with the shopping safely tucked away in the boot. The rain had begun to fall more heavily as they had packed the last of the bags away, and now the windscreen wipers were struggling to clear the screen from the deluge that fell from the sky.

Frances laughed. 'A typical autumn day! July was OK but wasn't August terrible? I've been hoping for an Indian summer but it doesn't look like that's going to happen.'

'The stream at the bottom of my garden was flooded half the time,' said Janet. 'I thought it was going to come into the bit I call my proper garden.' She laughed and said, 'I used to go and put a stick in every day just like Pooh did. But I was never stranded. I didn't have to sit on a branch with my pots of honey!' She sighed and continued, 'I remember summer as long, hot days with blue skies and never a thought of rain.'

Frances nodded and said, 'I remember being able to go swimming in the outdoor pool and having endless doll's tea parties on the lawn dressed only in my knickers!'

They both smiled at their memories and

Janet said, 'I can't tell you how lovely it is to not have to catch the bus home – especially in this! I would have been soaked.'

They pulled up in the driveway of a small bungalow. It was at the far end of the village from Janet and she never came this way now she didn't have a car. The net curtain at the front twitched and a grey-haired man peered out. He let the curtain drop and a moment later the front door opened. The man appeared; a stick clutched in one hand. He waved it at Frances and shouted crossly, 'Where have you been, girl? I expected you ages ago.' He flourished his stick again and added scornfully, 'Gossiping, I suppose.'

Frances got out of the car. 'Now then, Dad. Don't be grumpy. I've been no longer than I said I'd be. And look who I've met! It's Janet! Do you remember her from the library? Janet, meet Arthur.'

He peered at her and smiled with recognition. 'Of course I remember. Fancy that. Come on in. Come on, Frances, do get a move on. Don't leave us all standing in the rain.'

'OK, OK.' Frances grinned ruefully at Janet and said, 'Let me get the shopping in, Dad.'

Frances opened the boot and pulled out

three bags. Janet took one of them and they went inside.

In a living room, crowded with photographs and knick-knacks, they sat drinking tea. Frances' dad had fallen asleep and was snoring gently in his chair, his mouth open. Rain streamed down the windows and Janet felt more at peace than she had for ages. Frances handed her a plate of ginger biscuits and Janet took one.

'Mmm, nice,' Janet said. 'I used to love these when I was little. I still remember the village grocer's. Especially on shopping days. The biscuits were kept in open-topped tins by the counter and the grocer used to save the broken ones for me. The shop was bursting with smells. I used to love going in there, just to sniff, while Mum did the shopping. Everything had its own smell – roasting coffee beans, cheese on the counter, the biscuits, spices and tea.'

'How wonderful,' said Frances. 'The supermarket doesn't smell of anything, does it?'

'It's a wonder they don't pipe it in, along with that awful music,' said Janet. 'It's all so impersonal. Not like Mr Dunn in his white coat behind the counter, smiling and knowing everything there was to know about the people he served. He was like an uncle.'

'It's another world to me,' said Frances. 'Almost before my time. Anyway, what are you doing now? Did you say you were retired? We moved away a few years ago and I'm only back now to look out for Dad. Mum died and now he's on his own he needs help with the shopping and odd jobs, so I try to get over every couple of weeks.'

'It was after my mother died that I was able to move here. I looked after her for years and, with the money she left me, I suddenly decided that I wanted a complete change. So I moved out to a little house down the lane by the church.'

'It sounds wonderful,' said Frances. 'Lucky you. Have you got any family of your own?'

'No,' said Janet. 'I was too busy working and looking after Mum and Dad.' She looked round at the photographs. Frances smiled out from family groups: two boys and a girl; a huge man with one hand resting on her shoulder. Janet wasn't going to own up to the real reason she had never married. Nobody would ever have said of Frances, 'God forgot what he was doing when he made you'.

Janet had been thirteen when one of her mother's friends had said it. Janet had then gone away and studied her face in the mirror. It was true, she decided. Her nose was too big, her eyelashes and eyebrows too pale, her eyes were hidden behind thick glasses and her hair was thin and mousy. After that she had walked with her head down, afraid of seeing revulsion in other people's faces.

And always the thought, *Who would want to marry me?*

Frances sighed. 'I'm never going to be able to retire like that. Not with my career path!' She laughed and added, 'I love it really, but how nice to have all that freedom.'

Janet looked at her. Suddenly she was fed up with pretending. 'It isn't,' she said. 'I thought it would be but it isn't. I get up every morning because that's what one does. But I don't know what to do with myself. I can't afford to run the car so I have no transport. My knee often hurts and it's hard to walk anywhere. I'm always cross with myself for feeling so miserable. I'm only sixty-two but I feel about ninety. My neighbour's husband was killed in 9/11 and I can't make sense of the world any more. I suppose it took me back to remembering the war – all the tragedies that I only came to understand when I was older – and how it was supposed to be the war to end all wars.'

Arthur stirred in his chair and said, 'Can I have another cup of tea then?' He hauled himself to his feet and brought his cup across for a refill. Frances poured from the big brown teapot and added milk. Arthur grabbed a teaspoon and added three large spoons of sugar. 'That's one of my legacies from the war,' he said. 'Sugar. As much of it as I want, when I want.'

Frances laughed and said, 'It's a wonder you don't look like the Michelin Man, Dad.'

Arthur peered across at Janet and asked, 'What do you remember of the war then?'

'I remember our house was hit by a doodlebug. We were lucky not to be killed, Mum used to say. It was only because we had gone to visit her sister that we weren't in it when it was hit. We stayed with her for a while and then moved just down the road.'

'That must have been awful – losing your home,' said Frances.

'I was too young to remember really. I can remember going back and seeing the house in ruins. All I wanted was my doll. I think that was what the war meant to me. Hitler had killed my Angelica. Mum got me another one from somewhere but I never loved her the same.' There were tears in her eyes and Frances moved over to give her a hug.

From the chair by the fire, Arthur spoke. 'Never give up hope, lass. You must never give up hope.'

'He's right, Janet. Come on, let's get you and your shopping home before your frozen bits melt. I'd love to see your house and perhaps I could see you next time I'm over to see Dad?'

'Oh, that would be wonderful. Please, do.'

Frances reached into her bag and pulled out a pen and an old envelope. 'Here, I'll write down my address and phone number. We can keep in touch.' She got up and Janet followed her out.

From the doorway Frances' dad shouted, 'Remember what I said, lass!'

Janet shouted back, 'I will!'

That night she fell quickly asleep for the first time in months. Lights and the slam of a car door disturbed her and she woke.

It was three o'clock in the morning.

She sat up in bed, terrified. There was never any traffic at this time of night. Dreadful thoughts of burglars came to her and she felt she would faint with fright. She thought she ought to phone the police but hiding under the bedclothes felt preferable.

'Pull yourself together, Janet,' she said firmly to herself and got out of bed to see what was going on. She couldn't see much from her own room but the spare room on the other side of the house afforded a view of Lou's driveway. Trees and the hedgerow gave her only a partial view, but she could see that there were two cars there and one of them was a police car.

Perhaps Lou had burglars and had phoned for the police? Or, had she had an accident?

But no, there she was, getting out of her car holding something in her arms whilst a man opened the front door. Janet couldn't see what it was, but Lou was handling it very carefully. Another man got out of the police car and followed them in.

At least it wasn't any of those terrifying scenarios her imagination had conjured up. She yawned and went back to the warmth of her bed.

Sleep didn't come easily though, and Janet slipped in and out of dreams featuring masked men and police chases down the lane with blue lights flashing and gunfire.

Through it all she knew that she needed to rescue Lou, who was carrying a bundle in her arms, but she didn't know what to do. She gave up the attempt at sleep at half-past six, deciding she might as well get up, get something done in the garden and make the most of what promised to be a dry day. An hour later she was dressed and finishing off her breakfast when she heard a car on the lane.

Curiosity got the better of her. She grabbed her old coat from its hook beside the back door and pulled on her gardening shoes. A herbaceous border backed on to Lou's drive and if she went and did some weeding at the back she would be able to see what was going on.

A man got out of the car and rang the doorbell. The door opened and he went in. Janet was just going to go back inside, thinking she might be there all day, when the door opened again and Lou came out, followed by the man. She carried a shallow cardboard box. The man took it from her and as it changed hands, Janet saw what was inside. A small furry head emerged from the folds of a towel. The cat opened its mouth and a tiny mew came out.

Janet was horrified. Here there was no

voice of common sense. Only panic. A cat! Was Lou going to have a cat? Visions of being incarcerated in her own home in case she met up with it outside, of her precious birds unable to come into the garden, of not being able to garden, of not being able to feed the birds any more, filled her with horror. She stumbled back into the house, her heart pounding and her breath rapid. It was a nightmare.

Nine

Lou watched as Flyer was carried out of the room by one of the nurses. He turned his face up to her as he went – his eyes barely open – as if begging her to stay with him and not to leave him alone amongst complete strangers. Already she felt as if he were her cat: bonded to him by the time they had shared the night before, their mutual needs. The thought that he might not survive was unbearable and she sought reassurance again.

'Don't you think his chances might be

better than fifty-fifty?' she asked Jake hopefully. 'He did survive the night and he's such a fighter.'

Jake grunted. 'I still think it's touch and go with him. And, to be honest, I'm still not convinced it's fair on him to operate, to put him through more traumas. Those wounds in his shoulder are a mess and I'm very concerned about his back legs.'

'You will try though, won't you?'

'I will. But have you thought that somebody might be missing him?'

Ray interrupted, 'I'll put a notice in the Lost and Found section of the local paper if you like. If the owners see it they can get in touch with the police station,'

'Oh, would you?' said Lou. 'Thanks.' She paused and added, 'I know it's awful of me but I really hope that the owners don't see it.'

'Hmm,' said Jake. 'It's a hard thing to lose a pet and not know what has happened to it.'

Lou frowned. 'I'm sure it is.' She couldn't explain to either of them the depth of her longing for the little animal. They were probably thinking that if she really wanted a cat there were plenty of others in the world for her to choose from. Nevertheless, she knew that this was the one for her, as surely as she had known that she and Johnny belonged together. She didn't want him to be taken from her too.

'If you're really sure. Remember that it's going to be expensive and he might not pull through.' He paused. 'I still think it might be better, kinder—'

Lou interrupted, 'I've already told you I'll pay, no matter what. Is that the problem – that you think I might not fork out if he does die?' She glared at him, a bright patch of red on each cheek.

He raised his hands and said, 'OK, OK. I'll do it.' He looked at Ray and raised his eyebrows as though to say, *Look what you've landed me with. Thanks, mate!* 'Phone me this afternoon,' he said to Lou, and handed her a card with the practice details on it. 'We'll need to do some blood tests and I may not operate until tomorrow. I'll get some fluids into him and some antibiotics before we start so that he's a bit stronger.'

'Are you sure he's a good vet?' Lou asked Ray when they were outside.

He laughed. 'Oh, yes. He's the best. He's just a bit grumpy.'

Lou said indignantly, 'A bit...? A lot, I would say. We seemed to do nothing but argue.' She went on, 'I know it's silly, but I feel as if I'm abandoning the kitten. He must find everything so strange and very, very frightening.'

'Animals seem to adapt. They adapt better than people do, I think,' Ray said as he unlocked the car with the remote control. The car park was almost empty. The car alongside Ray's contained a small dog that barked at them as they approached. 'We don't know what goes on inside their heads. I often think my Mum's dog is summing us all up and deciding people are pretty odd. If he were a judge he'd be a hanging judge – I'm sure we don't come up to his expectations. He sits and looks at me sometimes as though he's trying to tell me something, and then sighs and walks off.'

He helped Lou into the car and passed her the seat belt. 'Look. It's my day off and I've not had breakfast yet.'

'Neither have I,' Lou said. 'Just that cup of coffee you made me. Though I do still feel quite full from that massive breakfast I had in the middle of the night!'

'I've nothing much to do today,' Ray said, seeing the hours ahead looming emptily. It had only been ten days since Jenny had announced her plan to change jobs and move to Scotland. She had gone without a backward look, as though their relationship had meant nothing. He was glad that the ring he had bought for her was still on his bedside table at home; the question he had been going to ask still only a hope in his heart. With the passing of each day he had slowly begun to realize that it was for the best, that they had little in common, but he still missed her. He hoped, desperately, that Lou would agree to help him fill in some of the empty hours.

'Why don't we go back to the café?' he said. 'It will only take twenty minutes and you can meet Grace – the other half of the partnership.'

'I'd like to meet her,' Lou said. 'They intrigue me. I can't imagine being stuck there all day.'

'They make good money,' Ray said. 'The place has a great reputation and they get people coming off the motorway to go there, instead of using the service station.'

The little diner was packed, and the car park beside it was filled with trucks and two Freightliners, which took up much of the space. Grace waved to them as they came in, but she was too busy to talk. They sat, silent, watching the customers tuck away vast quantities of food.

After a while, Grace brought them mugs of coffee. 'Have these on the house. I hope you don't mind waiting ... It feels like a conspiracy plan – that nine hundred drivers have all made a pact to come here at the same time.' She ran her fingers through her hair and struck a dramatic pose. 'Back to your kitchen, wench!'

She was as small as Meg was big – a tiny woman with soft, blonde hair framing her face and lying on her shoulders, and an impish smile. Her blue T-shirt proclaimed that only boring women had tidy kitchens. It was half an hour before she came back to take their orders. 'I'm sorry,' she said. 'It's been one of those mornings.' She looked at them both and smiled at Lou. 'My guess is you're the young lady Meg told me about?' Lou nodded, and Grace continued, 'I gather you had a rough time with an unwelcome visitor. I hope it didn't upset you too much.'

'No,' said Lou. 'It was horrible at the time, but Ray and Don saw me home safely. And Venn came to the rescue.' She watched as a large German Shepherd dog sauntered across the room, stretched and lay down beside Grace.

‘Meet Colonel. He’s *my* guardian,’ Grace said.

The dog raised his head to her patting hand.

‘We had another adventure on the way back,’ Ray said, and told Grace about the kitten.

‘Poor little mite,’ she said. ‘I bet you want to keep him. You must be worried about him.’

‘I am,’ said Lou. ‘I just want the day to be over, to know that he’s OK.’ She ran her fingers through her hair and yawned. ‘I’m sorry. I suddenly feel exhausted.’

Ray looked at her. ‘You do look tired. Why don’t I take you home? I can come back for my breakfast after I’ve dropped you off.’

‘Would you? I feel too tired to eat anything. But haven’t you got other things to do?’

‘Not me,’ said Ray. ‘It’s my day off and I can’t think of a better way of spending it than here with Grace.’ He winked at Grace and she winked back, a cheeky smile on her face. ‘I’ll be back in an hour. And then I shall really be ready for that breakfast of yours.’

It was ready for him when he returned; the place was now fairly quiet. Grace came and joined him. 'Where does she live? I'm sure I've seen her in here before. She must have been with her husband. What a tragedy.'

Ray looked at her. 'What do you mean?'

'Didn't she tell you?'

'No. Tell me what?'

'Meg told me Lou was on the road yesterday because she had been to her husband's memorial service. He was killed in 9/11.'

Ray gasped. 'God. No. How dreadful.' He thought of the photograph he had seen in her living room, and suddenly understood her need for the kitten. He decided not to put the advertisement in the local paper after all. There was no harm in the small conspiracy and he hoped the kitten's previous owner would not begrudge the concealment if they found out.

Ten

Flyer was aware of hands that held him, that carried him, that laid him on a table. He was aware of a needle that stabbed him, and then of lying on a soft blanket, looking out through wire, shut away from the world in a big box. He felt too ill to care. Every part of him hurt. There were other animals near. He could hear them breathing – one of them mewing loudly, protesting at his own imprisonment, as he awaited neutering.

Opposite Flyer, face forlorn, a dog injured in a road accident was recovering from surgery. He whimpered: wanting his owners, wanting to be away from this strange place that smelled so odd. Flyer was aware of the dog's misery. It echoed his own.

Everything was wrong. The familiar smells of farmyard, barn, the countryside around and the kitchen and the humans he knew were replaced by strange smells – unpleasant smells – he wanted to escape from. It was an alien environment, and he longed for the feel of Zannie's hands on his fur – smoothing, scratching between his ears, rubbing the soft fur of his belly.

He wanted the sounds of sheep and cattle, the stamp of a horse in the stable and the feel of straw beneath him. He slept fitfully, waking to pain but falling asleep again, aware of constant attention. The people were kind and they were gentle, but they were not *his* people.

He woke to the noise of his cage door being opened. He was lifted gently, carried out of the room and into another, and laid on a table. Bright lights shone down on him. Hands held him, and a strange object was put over his face. He slid into oblivion.

'If he makes it, I'll be amazed,' Jake, the vet, said. 'I hope he does. His finder was very anxious to keep him.' He paused and scratched his head, adding, 'Though I'm not convinced she's the best person for the job.'

He put the X-ray film on to the light box and pointed at the pelvis. 'Look.' he said to Alison, the practice nurse. 'He's broken it on two sides. That's what's the matter with his rear end. I thought it might be. With the breaks where they are we can leave it and hopefully it will heal by itself. He'll be slow to get back on his feet though. The worst fear is of the damage that might have been done to the nerves. We won't know for a while whether everything is going to be working properly.'

He started working on the shoulder wounds – shaving fur, stitching torn muscle and finally closing the ragged skin tears. He found, once he started operating, that he too was anxious that the kitten should live. It would be a miracle considering the state he was in. What he must have been through to survive...

An hour later, Flyer was back in his cage. He began to surface, feeling dizzy, unable to understand this strange sensation.

'Hey, little feller,' said a soft voice. It was Alison, who had noticed his movement. 'So, you're back with us, are you? I wonder how you'll fare tonight.'

Flyer did not like the feeling in his shoulders, nor the pain in his hindquarters. His front paw was shaved and a tube ran into it, which had been taped to hold it in place. He followed the tube to where it ended in a bag outside the cage. He wanted to tear it out but didn't have the energy. He didn't have the energy even to yowl. He did not like the hospital room, or the other animals in cages around him. He did not like the odd sensation when he tried to stand and how everything seemed to whirl round him.

He tried again to stand. He could not understand why his legs betrayed him. He watched as the cage door opened, and then came a sharp prick that hurt but took away the pain. He closed his eyes to shut out this strange world.

He slept and dreamed he was playing a game of chase – trying to catch the retriever's tail. He woke, needing Haddock. He would not touch the food that was put in front of him. Again, hands lifted him and fluid dripped into his throat. He had no strength to protest.

'He might make it,' Jake said, looking down at the kitten. 'We'd better keep him here until he's on his feet again. It's going to be a few days before he's ready to leave.'

'How old do you think he is?' asked Alison.

'I'd guess around four months. He's not even half-grown yet. If he had been a little bigger the bird might have thought less of attacking him.'

Later that afternoon Lou phoned, refreshed from a long sleep. 'How is he?' she asked anxiously.

'He's still alive,' said Jake. 'I've stitched his shoulder wounds. But he has a fractured pelvis.'

'Oh no,' said Lou, 'that sounds awful.'

'It might be, I'm afraid. The bones usually heal well but the worst danger is if his organs or nerves have been damaged and it affects his bowels and bladder.'

'What can you do if that happens?'

'Not much. It depends how bad it is. I want to keep him here for a week to ten days to make sure he has recovered and he's in full working order.'

'That's fine,' said Lou with relief. 'Can I phone every day for a bulletin?'

'Of course,' said Jake.

By the end of the day Flyer had stopped feeling dizzy, though he couldn't bear to stand on his back legs when he tried. It was easier to lie down and not move at all. His world had been reduced to nothing but pain. It tore through him, throbbing in the skin and muscle of the shoulders where the talons had gripped him; a dull ache pounded in his broken bones. The only part of him that didn't hurt was his tail. He wanted to swear and lash it in protest but all he could manage was a faint grumble and a twitch of the very tip. At least it was something.

For two days he refused to eat. Alison used a syringe to drop glucose water with Rescue Remedy into his mouth every hour. He swallowed, but did not attempt to lap.

She spent time trying to tempt him with different foods, without success. On the third day, however, the food set in front of him had a new flavour. He had never had cod mixed with tinned sardines. He licked tentatively and then savoured the taste, leaving a clean dish.

She stroked his head, delighted, and said, 'At last! Good boy! We've found something you like.'

The dog opposite had gone home and a small cat was in its place. He, too, hated his cage, the unfamiliar room and the other animals around him. He swore at Flyer, who couldn't be bothered to swear back. Flyer turned his back to the room and the bright lights and lay there, feeling forlorn and lonely.

That evening Jake helped him on to his litter tray. That was new to him. Farm cats were expected to go outside when necessary, but urgency – and the smell of the tray, which had been sprayed with a toilet-training aerosol – signalled its use to him.

Jake sighed with relief. That was another worry out of the way – at least for the moment. Everything was working as it should.

Jake went to look at the cat before evening surgery on Saturday. It was five days since Flyer had first been brought in. 'He's certainly tough,' Jake said. 'I think there's a good chance he'll recover.'

The door shut behind the last patient – the black Labrador almost dragging his owner out of the door, so glad was he to escape that dreadful place. Alison came out of the dispensary and asked, 'Ready for tea, Jake?'

He looked at her and said, 'I certainly am. Would you like to join us? You look exhausted.'

'That would be great,' said Alison. 'I can help you cook it if you like. You've had a busy day too.' She loved the thought of the two of them cooking together in the kitchen. It made her daydreams feel less fanciful. Why shouldn't he fall in love with her and want to marry her? She might only be nineteen, and plain and dumpy, but she had no doubt about her ability to replace his dead wife and be a mother to his daughter, Susie.

'OK,' said Jake. 'Thanks.'

They finished checking the animals in the hospital and climbed the stairs to Jake and Susie's rooms, which were on the first floor. Alison lived on the second floor of the rambling old house. She had moved in six months ago when Jake's partner in the practice had left.

In the kitchen, Susie sat at the table with her homework books in front of her. She looked up and scowled at Alison. 'What's she doing here?' she grumbled.

Jake said, struggling to keep his temper, 'I've asked her to have tea with us. All right?'

'No, it's not all right,' shouted Susie. 'We never get any time together – just the two of us. Why can't she go back to her own flat and leave us alone?'

Jake snapped, 'Because we're both tired, Susie, and it helps both of us.'

Susie glared at him, and said in a small, tight voice, 'Well, it doesn't help me.' She swept her books from the table and into her school bag, pushed her chair back and stormed out of the room.

Alison watched her go and said, 'Forget it, Jake. I'll leave you to it.'

Jake said, 'No, don't let her bully you. She'll be back when she smells the food.'

Alison hesitated, biting at her lower lip.

'Perhaps I should go, Jake. It must be hard for her. It is only a year since her mum died.'

He sighed. 'I know, I know. Maybe I am being hard on her, but I'm so tired all the time. It's unrelenting. Busy all day, call-outs at night, hardly any sleep. God, why did Alistair have to go and fall in love with an Australian girl who wouldn't live over here?'

'Well, love has its own rules, doesn't it,' she said ruefully. *If only he'd notice me*, she thought, *and see me as a desirable woman instead of his employee*. 'Maybe someone will answer your advertisement and you'll have a new partner soon.'

'If only...' groaned Jake as the phone rang.

Jake was called out again in the middle of the night. Whenever this happened Jake buzzed Alison and she came down to sleep in the spare room so that Susie wasn't alone. Susie always hated it – resenting the fact that her father had left her in the middle of the night, and resentful of Alison.

That night, after the row at teatime and a disrupted evening, she raged at Alison, 'Why does he have to go out? Why can't he stay here and go out in the morning?'

'Because he can't leave an animal to suffer. They don't know what time of day it is. He just has to go; that's his job.'

Susie refused to listen, clapping her hands over her ears and ignoring Alison. 'I want him here with me, I want him here with me, I don't want you, I don't want you,' she chanted.

Alison felt like slapping the child. It wasn't fair on Jake and it wasn't fair on her. Life wasn't fair and Susie needed to learn it. But then that was the problem. Susie had already learned that life wasn't fair when her mother died of cancer and this was Susie trying to come to terms with it. Alison could not imagine how she would have dealt with losing her own mother at that age. It didn't bear thinking about.

Susie buried her head under the duvet and Alison went back to the spare room, wondering what on earth she could do to help.

Breakfast was no better – Jake exhausted after hardly any sleep and Susie bad-tempered. Alison heard the shouting and was glad that Sunday was her day off, once she had checked the animals. She went into the hospital and opened Flyer's cage to see how he was doing.

Flyer, recovering, recognized Alison's unhappiness as she checked him over. He licked her hand, and managed a token purr. He patted her face with a gentle paw. Few of the animals she nursed did more than suffer her and his action was comforting. The physical contact was soothing, and she began to relax as she stroked his soft fur.

Jake came up behind her and looked at the cat. Flyer's blue eyes looked back at them both. 'He's Siamese,' Jake said, 'so we're probably in for some fun when he's strong enough to use his voice. It's enough to wake the dead when a Siamese yowls!'

Alison knew that. They were often noisy patients, though few people owned them in their practice. 'Do you think he'll recover?'

'He's determined and he was very healthy when he was taken. I'm beginning to think that there's every chance. I suspect he's a terrific character. There's something about him.'

Flyer listened to them, staring up at Jake. He was beginning to feel better. He had to accept what was happening. He had been plunged into a totally new existence, and his instinct told him that all he had known before was gone for ever.

Outside, rain lashed against the window. The wind whistled round the house and Alison thought of a cosy day curled up with a book in front of the fire.

Jake said, 'Susie has asked if her friend Pete can come over for the day.'

'What did you say?' asked Alison anxiously. Neither of them liked the boy but Susie seemed to. Round-faced and stocky, he looked harmless enough, but neither of them trusted him. He had been after school a couple of times, wanting to see round the surgery and look at the animals. But his questions had been peculiar – more about how much blood there was when they operated than about the animals themselves.

'I've said yes,' replied Jake. 'I know how lonely she is and I know I'm going to have to make a couple of farm visits today. I'll leave them some sandwiches for lunch but could you keep an eye on them for me?'

Alison saw her quiet day disappearing. She began to wonder if the arrangement they had was as good as it had first seemed. No rent and no bills to pay in return for accommodation ... and what was beginning to feel like constant child-minding. Two jobs, not one. Oh well. It was worth it. And if she and Jake were to marry then that would still be what she'd have to do. If only Susie showed some sign of liking her.

* * *

Pete arrived at Susie's house in the late morning. For a while, he and Susie played a game on her computer, but it was too childish for his tastes. He wished his mother would buy him one of the games rated eighteen. That would be brilliant. He'd seen them in the shops; blood and guns and shooting and stalking were much more fun than silly platform games. Making little cartoon characters jump up ladders and try to catch gold coins on the way was kid's stuff. What he *really* wanted to do was see the animals in the hospital. He wished he could watch the operations.

The hospital was out of bounds and Susie knew it. She tried to argue with Pete but he wouldn't listen. She knew what he was capable of doing if she resisted and, in the end, there was nothing she could do. He knew the way and there was nobody to stop them.

'Wouldn't it be fun to let them out?' Pete said, and pushed Susie out of the way when she protested. He went across to Flyer and opened his cage door.

Susie watched in horror. There would be terrible trouble and he might cause serious damage. Even she knew they had to be very careful with the recovering animals.

Pete put his hand into Flyer's cage and grabbed him by the neck where talons had ripped skin and muscle. The stitched wounds were still very sore and the pain of being grabbed was excruciating.

Nobody had ever treated the young cat like this.

Pete's hands were hard, and he was hurting the cat deliberately. He grinned; he was always glad when he inflicted pain. Susie had told no one of his pinches and hair pulling, the kicks and punches, and the ever-present threat of violence from him.

She wanted to stop him. Her father would be furious with her. But she was too afraid of the boy. Panic seized her. Why on earth had she asked him to come over?

Because he had told her what he would do if she didn't.

Pete knew Susie was mostly on her own at the weekends, and that everyone was too busy for her. His own parents were divorced; his father remarried and with a new baby. His mum was always on at him and was worse since his father left. He didn't like his new stepmother either, though he had to spend alternate weekends with his father.

He revelled in the knowledge that his stepmother was afraid of him, and that she did her best to ensure they were never left alone together and, even more importantly, that he was never left alone with his baby step-sister. It amused him to behave perfectly when his father was with them so that he never realized his son's potential. He knew that his mother occasionally rang his father and told him about their son's behaviour, but he also knew that his father thought his ex-wife was becoming paranoid about the boy, and doing her best to spoil his new relationship.

His new wife dared not say what she felt. Stepmothers were notorious for not liking an inherited child.

The voices went on in Pete's head:

'Peter, don't do that.'

'Peter! I said, did you hear me?'

'Wash your hands, clean your teeth and get your gym kit ready for school. Go to bed. Get up. Do your homework. Are you listening to me? Don't you look at me like that!'

Flyer, enraged by pain, flung out his good paw, claws unsheathed, and caught Pete on his bare arm, making a livid trail of angry scratches, along which bright beads of blood welled and dripped.

Pete yelled with pain and dropped the cat – fortunately only on to the floor of his cage.

Flyer had intended harm, and the scratches were deep. He removed his hand fast and Susie raced across and shut the door. She could do nothing about the drip, which had come out, but perhaps they would think it had happened when the cat scratched. She was glad that the cat had done so but was afraid to show it.

Alison raced into the hospital when she heard the noise. She hadn't realized Susie and Pete had gone into the little hospital room. Heaven knew what had happened now.

Jake had just returned from the last visit and he walked in to see what the noise was about. He took in the scene: Pete with blood streaming from his arm, Flyer swearing in his cage and the drip dangling loose. Susie looked terrified.

His first thought was for the cat. He bent to look at the creature, noting blood welling in the stitches on his shoulder. It didn't take much to work out what had happened. He turned and looked at his daughter and said, his voice like ice, 'You can go to your room. I'll talk to you later.'

Susie fled, tears streaming. He had never used that tone of voice with her before. She wanted to run away, find a new home, have her mother back. It wouldn't have happened if Mum had been here.

Jake said to Alison, 'Take Pete into the kitchen and bathe his arm. Phone his mother. He can go. Now.' He looked at Pete. 'And you. You never, ever come here again. Do you hear me?'

Once they had all gone he took the kitten out and examined him. The little animal trembled, obviously still shaken by the attack on him. Jake cursed them both. The cat seemed unharmed but he worried that the shock might undo all the progress he had made. He stroked the little cat gently, and then put him back into the cage.

Flyer retreated to the back of the cage immediately, and watched with wary eyes as the man closed the door.

Jake sighed and went to find Susie. She was lying on her tummy on her bed, her shoulders heaving. He stood by the door and said, 'What on earth were you doing in there? You know you aren't to go into the hospital.'

'That beastly cat scratched him,' Susie said, avoiding the question because she was afraid of landing Pete in trouble.

'And what exactly was he doing to the cat? There's no way that cat would hurt anyone unless he was badly hurt too,' he told Susie.

Susie avoided his eyes, wondering if it was possible to be even more miserable. And what would Pete do on Monday when they were both back at school? She was not sure who frightened her more – Pete or her father. She knew her father was very angry.

Jake looked down at her. She was small and slender, and her hair was cut short now because he never had time to help her plait it for school. Blonde tendrils clung to her face and the brown eyes that looked up at him held all the terror of a trapped animal. She was so like her mother, and he wouldn't hurt her whatever she had done. She was alone too often. He had failed her. He felt he had also failed the little cat. He should have obeyed his instinct and refused to allow Pete to visit.

Susie managed to find her voice. 'Daddy ... I didn't want to bring Pete here. He made me.'

'How? How could he do that?'

She could not hide her fear of him any longer. 'He likes hurting.' She pushed back the sleeve of her jersey, revealing bruises that Pete had inflicted on her because she had tried to defy him.

Jake looked at her. She had the same

expression in her eyes as the cat. Terror. He was appalled. He rolled back his daughter's other sleeve. This arm was even worse. He was overcome with fury. He had to do something about the little brute. But what? How did you ensure a bully stopped his torment?

'Susie...' His voice broke. He put his arms round her, holding her tight. He never had enough time for her. What could he do to make amends? Sunlight came through the window, highlighting her hair, so like her mother's. Memory still hurt, and his anger at Fate dominated him. He could lose himself in work but what could Susie do? It had been so short a time since Eileen died. Cancer infuriated him. He battled it too often in his patients. So often you could alleviate it, even subdue it, or force it into remission. At other times, no matter how you fought, it was the winner. Eileen had been determined not to lose. But it had made no difference.

He held Susie tightly. She had suffered as much as he had during those last weeks. He had a sudden flashback – of standing outside the little room at the hospice with their doctor, at the beginning of that last week. He couldn't bear watching his wife slowly ...

too slowly ... lose her fight. And how she had fought.

'If I allowed a dog to suffer like that I'd be considered guilty,' Jake had said to her doctor.

Steve, the doctor, had sighed. 'There's never an easy way out,' he had said. 'Do you think I don't agonize too?'

Jake cursed the memory. He had been wrapped up in his own grief, and had hardly spared a thought for his daughter. 'Susie, I need to make sure that Pete didn't damage the little cat more. He's been very badly injured. He almost died. I'm still not sure he's going to pull through. Let's take him into the surgery and have a look at him. Yes?' He nuzzled his face in her hair and his arms were strong about her.

Susie suddenly felt safe – safer than she had for a long time. She nodded; her voice was not yet under control and tears were too near the surface.

Jake opened the cage door.

Flyer looked up at him, distrust in his eyes. Was this man going to grab him and hurt him, although he had been gentle before? The man's soft voice was soothing. Flyer relaxed and the panic died out of his eyes.

Jake sighed with relief. Shock could do more damage than injuries. He hated losing a patient and this little one had had a very bad time in the past couple of days. Maybe they could dispense with the drip now. It had come out easily, so no major harm had been done.

'Look. I know we don't have enough time together,' he said to Susie. 'Would you like to come with me on my rounds to the farms when you're home? I'm sure they'll always find room for you in the kitchen and maybe someone can take you to see the animals. I'll be busy when we get there, but you won't be alone. Sometimes you might be able to help me. Would you like that?'

Susie nodded. She had always longed for this, but had never liked to ask her father. Maybe she could feed baby lambs and play with new kittens. There were always tiny animals on a farm.

Jake carried the little cat into the surgery.

Flyer lay still in his arms, afraid of what might follow. The boy's rough treatment had frightened and hurt him and he was no longer sure he could trust those about him. Nobody had ever harmed him before.

'There, little feller, you're safe now.'

The voice was soothing, the hands that

held him gentle. Flyer felt the needle slip in, and then the pain eased.

'Stroke him,' Jake said, sitting on the chair he kept for clients who came in with their dogs for small treatments like claw cutting and anal gland relief. 'Pete may have taught him to distrust everyone. Often it only needs one bad experience to last a lifetime. He needs to learn he can trust us.'

Susie stroked the soft fur. The little cat looked up at her. He gave a token purr. His blue eyes looked into hers, as if he was trying to tell her something. Susie felt a sudden, overwhelming hope that he would survive. Maybe if the lady who found him didn't want him she could keep him. Something alive of her own to love and hug.

Flyer was glad to return to his cage and cuddle into the soft blanket. This time he kept well to the back, and crouched as if trying to make himself invisible every time anyone passed.

'I still have animals to help,' Jake said. 'We'll go to Mac's farm after lunch. There are some piglets there.' There was another chore to be done first, though and he was dreading it.

Listening to the ringing tone when he phoned Pete's mother, he half hoped she was out. He wondered how she would react when he explained what had happened to her son. She hadn't asked to see him when she had collected the boy and she needed to know. He hadn't anticipated indifference and it made him feel slightly less angry with the boy. It seemed he had his own burdens to bear. But Jake knew he would have to go and talk to the school about it. Pete needed to be stopped. He hoped that the scratches he had got might do the trick.

Susie, overwhelmed by what had happened and terrified that Pete would torment her on Monday when they went back to school, spent the rest of the day doing as she was asked. At Mac's farm she was greeted by the smiling farmer's wife, and spent the next half hour watching a litter of tiny piglets. When her father had finished his work she greeted him with a radiant smile of her own. 'They're so funny,' she said. 'But their mother doesn't like me.'

The sow had charged the railing surrounding her and her brood.

'She's protecting her babies,' Jake said with relief in his voice. Maybe life would improve.

'An apple pie for both of you,' the farmer's wife said, handing over a biscuit tin. She smiled at Susie. 'Make sure your dad brings you again. Next time there ought to be a little calf for you to see. And later in the month a new foal.'

Back at the surgery, Jake checked the cat again. He was trying to stand now, if only briefly, and he had eaten all of the food offered. All was well.

Flyer grew used to the nurse and to Jake; as his strength returned he rediscovered his voice. He demanded attention from everyone who passed, wanting company.

'I wish we could keep him,' Alison said. 'Susie loves him and so do I. Do you think his new owner's capable of looking after an injured animal? It will be weeks before he's fit again.'

Jake said, 'I know. I'm not sure either. I'll talk to her.'

He picked up the phone and asked Lou if she would come to the surgery. The kitten was nearly ready to leave the hospital and they needed to discuss his future.

Eleven

Susie was waiting in reception, hoping against hope that Lou would say she had changed her mind about having the cat. She had sat and cuddled him every day when she'd got home from school. He was surprisingly soothing.

Jake greeted Lou and sat down beside her. 'I'm really worried about you having him,' he said bluntly. 'I gather from Ray that you work as an accountant. You can't just leave him to fend for himself while you're out at work. Remember what I said. He needs to be kept confined and not allowed to jump so that his bones can mend. He'll need a lot of attention.'

She knew really that he was right to be asking, and that it showed professionalism, which continued beyond his own responsibilities and into the future of this patient. But she had already thought about it. Every day she had phoned to ask for a progress report and chatted with the practice nurse. Never Jake, because he was always busy.

But it was the way that he did it.

As though she was stupid, unthinking, selfish. She couldn't bear the thought of her newborn hopes being taken from her, of everything that she had finally dared to buy ending up in the dustbin.

She blazed up at him. 'You're so arrogant!' she said. 'Has it occurred to you that other people think things through? I can't believe you. You were almost determined not to operate on the animal and now he's getting better you still don't want me to have him. Not that it's any business of yours, but I have already handed my notice in at work and I'm going freelance. I'm taking holiday in lieu of notice.'

Never had she taken such a dislike to somebody so quickly. It was a long time since she had stuck her tongue out at anybody but she found an almost overwhelming urge to do it. What a boor he was.

Susie walked over, the cat in her arms. 'It was partly about your job, Lou. But it's my fault really, because I've fallen in love with him and I was sort of hoping you might change your mind.' She handed the cat over to Lou and stroked his head. 'Goodbye, puss. Be happy.' There were tears in her eyes.

Lou patted the chair next to her. 'Come and sit beside me and I'll tell you why he's so important to me. Perhaps you'll understand.'

Susie sat down, her hand again on the cat's back.

'It's like this.' She found it hard to tell her with Jake standing behind them, but she couldn't bear to see the child's unhappiness, feeling it in competition with her own. She drew a deep breath. 'I was married to a man called Johnny who I loved very much. He was killed in New York two years ago and I found this little scrap on the way back from a memorial service for him. Having him there in the house with me that night was almost the first time another living creature apart from me has been in the house since Johnny died. I wanted the cat to survive and live with me more than I have wanted anything since his death.' She looked at Susie. 'Can you understand that?'

Susie looked back and whispered, 'Yes. Yes, I can. My mum died last year from cancer. At least I've still got Daddy.'

Behind them, Jake cleared his throat. 'I tell you what,' he said. 'How about this? The animal does need an eye keeping on him for a while, to make sure his waterworks are still

OK. The stitches will need taking out too. I could pop in every day to make sure he's improving. You could come with me, Susie, and then you'll still be able to see him.'

Lou smiled at him. Perhaps she had misjudged him as much as he had misjudged her. 'Well, that would be great. I'm not that confident to be honest. It would be reassuring to have you call. And even when he's better, Susie, perhaps you would still like to come and cat-visit? It would be a pleasure to have you.'

Susie smiled with delight. She held the lid of the travel basket open and Lou placed the cat carefully inside. Susie scratched his head, said, 'See you later, little fellow,' and then closed the lid.

A plaintive wail came from inside the basket, as Lou picked it up to carry it out to the car. She couldn't believe it was finally happening – that the cat was coming home with her. She'd had a long conversation with Johnny, telling him all about it. How worried she was about looking after him properly, and about deciding to give up her job and go freelance. And always there was Johnny grinning, thumb up, saying, 'It'll be all right, Lou. You worry too much. It will be fine.'

* * *

Flyer crouched in his bed in the kitchen looking for danger. The big cage Lou had prepared for him sat on the floor in the corner. She had hung a blanket over the top of it to make it feel cosier. Inside was the most comfortable cat bed she could find, which was soft and lined with fleece. There was room for his water bowl and food bowl; a litter tray lay just outside the door. Gently, she lifted him from the travel basket and put him into the cage. What she would really have liked to do was cuddle him but she was nervous of hurting him, and afraid he might try to jump off her lap.

He had learned fear and he had lost trust. He needed to know his new surroundings, and identify the smells. All were strange to him. Lou knelt beside him, stroking him gently and talking to him. 'You'll be all right,' she whispered. 'I'll look after you.' The little cat watched every move she made as she walked round the kitchen, preparing a meal for them both. He had been eating well, Jake said, and she hoped that he would settle down soon.

The food smelled the same and that reassured him, especially when Lou put down a small bowl filled with steamed cod and sardines. He finished it, making sure every scrap had gone, and then tried to wash himself. His shoulders were still stiff and sore but he attempted a wash of sorts. It was not easy to balance, but he managed to lick his paw and wipe it over his face, and then decided he wanted to start exploring. The closed door of the cage stopped him and he yowled, scrabbling at it with a paw.

'No, puss,' said Lou. 'You've got to stay in there. It's for your own good.'

He yowled again and butted his head against the door. Lou sat down beside him, her own food on a plate in her hand. Flyer shot out a paw and hooked a piece of bacon off it.

'Hmm,' said Lou, 'you're definitely on the mend.'

Flyer crunched the crispy morsel and curled up close to Lou. He purred softly and she scratched his head for him.

Hanging on the wall was a cuckoo clock. She and Johnny had chosen it together from a shop that sold nothing else when they were on honeymoon in the Black Forest. Lou had been entranced. They had spent hours looking before emerging triumphant with their choice. It was a steep-roofed wooden chalet with fretted eaves and balcony, painted edelweiss and a little veranda. A man in a rocking chair supped from a huge glass of beer and a Saint Bernard dog nodded his head. A wooden pine tree stood to one side, against a picket fence. Long pine cone weights hung underneath and the brightly-painted cuckoo popped out of a little door between two upstairs windows. A treasured possession; winding it was the last thing she did every night.

It was midday and the tiny bird flew out and called twelve times. Flyer had never seen anything like it before. He crept back to his bed and sat, ears pricked and head on one side, his blue eyes wide. He stared up at the clock, waiting for the bird to come out again, and yowled several times, asking, 'What's that? Is it safe?'

Lou laughed and said, 'It's not going to hurt you, puss.' He behaved as if some dreadful monster lurked, ready to pounce. She wondered if it was normal cat behaviour, or if his abduction had made him wary.

Flyer crept to the front of his cage, staring up at the clock, puzzled when the bird vanished inside and the little door shut. He was desperate for comfort. Lou had fetched a huge cushion from upstairs and made a place for herself beside the cage, where he could see her. Once he had satisfied himself that nothing dangerous lurked to trap him, he wanted Lou's lap. He crouched beside the door, crying to be let out.

The continuing pleas broke Lou's heart and she opened the door to release him. She lifted him gently on to her lap. There he settled himself and purred, his small brown paws kneading. His presence was companionable, his need for her stirring her to feeling again. She had been numb for the past two years – unable to empathize with the people she met. Now she found herself considering the vet and his staff.

She had noticed Alison's longing, and wondered if Jake knew. He too would be affected by the recent death of his wife and not ready for new commitments. Susie must be missing her mother so much. She wondered if Jake had time for his daughter or was so immersed in his own feelings that he had forgotten she was grieving too.

Flyer was not prepared to be ignored. He reached up to touch her cheek, to remind Lou of his presence. He watched her, learning her, knowing she cared about him.

Lou felt a springing of hope, and with it came the thought that now was the time to decide on a name for him. A name would make him real and bring a sense of permanence about his presence, which was part of the belonging.

Ray, who had called in when he was off duty later that afternoon, sat drinking coffee and watching the animal. The kitten crouched in the safety of Lou's lap. He was wary of this new man whom he did not remember from the night they had picked him up.

'What shall I call him?' Lou asked. 'I keep calling him Puss, but that's not much of a name for such a character.'

Ray, sitting back nursing his mug of coffee, felt more relaxed than he had done since Jenny had left him. He liked Lou, and found her attractive. She was almost as tall as he was and, as he had suspected, she was indeed gorgeous. Grey eyed with delicately arched brows, carefully layered blonde hair with a side parting that left her clear-skinned forehead bare and a widely generous mouth. He wondered about her and the life she led, which to him seemed singularly lonely. 'Lucky?' he suggested, when she asked for ideas.

'Not right. I wonder what his previous owners called him?' she said with a frown. She felt a spurt of fear. 'Nobody's replied to the advert, have they?'

Ray's conscience twinged as he replied, 'No, don't you worry about that. And no one's reported a kitten missing. Goodness knows how far the bird flew before he dropped him.' He went on quickly, before she asked for more details, 'Can you manage him with your job?'

She grimaced. 'Don't you start. Jake was worried about that. But I've given it up. I've done it for two years and I'm tired of it,' she said. 'They gave it to me after Johnny died. I suppose they thought it might help me to be away from home. It was good at first, but hotels are lonely places. It seemed to emphasize the fact that mostly folk are couples, and I was always by myself.'

'What about family?'

'I haven't got any and Johnny's family don't want me. I suppose, too, I just realized that I'll never be able to make a new life for myself here if I'm always away with work. It suddenly feels like the time's right.'

'I'll get you some business cards done, if you like,' he said. 'What are you going to call yourself?'

'Lou Barton, Special Agent.'

They both laughed.

'That's what Johnny used to call me after we were married. I haven't decided yet.

Nothing fancy. Just my name, and maybe "specializing in farm accounts". I'm sure there is a need here, and I do know farming. My grandparents had a farm in Wiltshire and I often stayed with them. I loved those visits. I can do other accounts, of course, but I'd prefer those. If I keep it local I can choose my own timetable and need never leave him for long. Most of it would be done here.'

Flyer began to purr – without a lot of energy, but at least he was trying. He re-settled himself on Lou's lap and went to sleep.

'Could you leave him long enough to come out for a meal tonight?' Ray asked, ever hopeful.

She frowned and said, 'No, not yet. If Jake came calling and found me gone on his first night home, he would take him away immediately! Besides, Puss needs me to be here, and to be honest I need to be here too.' She looked at Ray's disappointed face and suggested, 'Maybe you could fetch a take-away? It would save me cooking. This little fellow does like to be cuddled. He never takes his eyes off me, and if I go out of the room he wails. It sounds so forlorn; I have not the heart to leave him. Poor little mite.

He's supposed to be kept in his cage but he has other ideas. I'm hoping that if I stay at floor level he can't come to much harm.'

Ray got up. 'I'll go now then. I'm hungry enough. Are you?'

Lou nodded. 'I am,' she said. 'I'll put some plates to warm and he can go back in his bed while we eat.'

Half an hour later the doorbell rang and, when she went to open it, there was Ray holding a plain, white carrier bag. 'Learn to fear the Greeks when they come bearing gifts,' he said with a smile.

'What sort of gift?' Lou asked and then caught the smell. 'Chinese! My favourite! Great! Bring it into the kitchen.'

From the kitchen came a raucous yell. They looked at each other in amazement. 'He's getting louder by the minute,' said Lou. 'I needn't worry about not knowing where he is when he's recovered!'

'Did he really make that din?' Ray asked. 'I've never heard anything like it.'

Lou laughed. 'Jake did say that a Siamese call could wake the dead,' she said. 'I can well believe it. He startled me almost out of my skin. Maybe I should name him Clarion. I think he's demanding to know why I have left him.'

They returned and Flyer greeted them eagerly. He lay on his side on the floor of his cage, his energy spent. He yowled again. 'Pick me up,' he said. 'Rescue me. I'm too tired to do it myself.'

Lou opened the door and stroked him. 'Come on, Puss. Go back to your bed. Why don't you have a sleep?'

'I'll put the food out for us.' Ray stared at the small animal, astonishment on his face, as the noise escalated. 'Does he want feeding too?'

'Not for a while,' Lou said. 'I've a feeling he's just yelling for me. He doesn't want to be left on his own. Poor scrap; he must still be in a lot of pain and maybe remembers being carried off. He must have been terrified. It was only a week ago, after all. And he has a whole new environment to get used to. Like being kidnapped.'

Ray dished several different portions of Chinese food on to the two plates. Lou's stomach rumbled. There was prawn fried rice, sweet and sour chicken, plain rice and noodles. No wonder he was such a big man! There was laughter in his blue eyes as he watched Lou's face. He said apologetically, 'Well, I was hungry. I hope you are!'

He had looked sad when they first met,

Lou thought. Out of uniform he wore navy blue corduroys and a home-made Aran sweater. 'My mum's an indefatigable knitter,' he had said when Lou admired the intricate pattern.

She put the kitten into his bed and sat down at the table. There was an indignant yowl and he struggled out of his bed. They both sat on the floor beside him and once again a slim, brown paw shot out to claw a piece of chicken from Ray's plate.

'He's a terror. Maybe it is a good job you got so much,' said Lou. 'He did that at lunchtime. He's determined to get his share! Nothing wrong with his appetite, is there?' She carried a heaped fork of noodles to her mouth. Again, the paw shot out to catch the dangling end and Lou pulled it away. 'It's no good. We're being too soft. He'll just have to grumble.'

They stood and carried their plates over to the table, Flyer protesting vigorously.

'You could name him Robber. Or Thief,' Ray said, laughing. 'You're going to have to watch that one or you'll lose all your own food.'

'Trojan ... Trooper ... he's lots of spunk. None of those sounds right. I wonder what he was called before.'

'Goodness knows,' Ray said. He took another piece of chicken off his plate and walked across the kitchen to bend and offer it to the kitten.

Flyer took it daintily and ate with delight. The food here was more interesting than he had on the farm, where cats had tinned food topped up with the mice they caught. Flyer then watched the people's lips intently, wondering what they were saying. It was a useless exercise. He yawned, then, with some difficulty, rearranged himself on his bed and finally went to sleep. He woke when the cuckoo came out of the clock and called the hour. He watched it, but had no desire to move. Moving still hurt, and he felt exhausted.

'We have to call him something,' Lou said after they had finished eating. 'Somehow names like Toby and Misty don't seem to suit him.'

'You could just carry on calling him Puss...'

'Certainly not,' said Lou. 'That's not a name for a cat with his history. He came here by flying ... we could call him Pilot, but that sounds like a dolphin! What about Flyer? Somehow it seems to suit him.'

'It sounds good to me,' Ray said. 'A little

unusual perhaps for something with four legs but there – so what!'

'Then Flyer it is,' Lou said. 'Came out of the sky, didn't you, little cat?'

Flyer was aching everywhere; the pain-killers he had had were wearing off. He sat and looked up at Lou, his eyes pleading. He yowled – long and low.

Lou frowned. 'Are you hurting, little one? I can't do anything about it at the moment. I'm sorry.' It was three hours before he was due for the next dose of painkillers. She hoped Jake might time his visit so that he could give it to him. What if she didn't manage to get it down him? 'I wish I knew what he's saying,' Lou said. 'He really does sound as if he's telling me something.'

Flyer snuggled down again, as if aware his pleas were useless.

'He'll be much better in a few days,' Ray said. 'I need to get home though. I'm due in early tomorrow.'

It seemed only moments after he had gone that the doorbell was ringing. Lou heaved a sigh of relief. Jake had come and could give the kitten his medicine. When she opened the door to let Jake in Susie bounced in after him, a big smile on her face.

'Come in,' said Lou. 'He's in the kitchen.

He's got a name now. Ray and I decided on one.'

'Ooh, what is it?' asked Susie.

'Flyer,' Lou replied. 'Because he flew to get here.'

They were greeted by a loud yowl. Flyer recognized their voices and stood slowly. He crept to the front of the cage and tried to rub against Susie's leg.

She bent to greet him, 'Hiya, Flyer.' She laughed. 'I'm a poet and I didn't know it!'

'He looks fine,' said Jake. 'How has he been?'

'Very nervous at first, but he has had something to eat. He also stole some of my lunch! He got tired very quickly though, and I think he's in a lot of pain.'

'Aye, he will be. It'll take him a week or two to get his energy back and a month or two for his pelvis to heal. Now, remember what I said about not letting him jump.'

'I won't,' said Lou, 'but he hates being in the cage. Would it matter if I let him out in the kitchen?'

'I'd try and keep him in there a couple of days at least,' said Jake. 'Give the bone a chance to heal a bit more. We don't want him trying to weight bear on it too much.' He looked round the kitchen and pointed,

'Is that his litter tray?'

'Yes,' said Lou.

'Hmm, the edges might be a little high for him to get on to. Do you have a shallower tray he can use for a while?'

'Oh, yes,' said Lou, 'I hadn't thought. That's a good idea. I'll do it now.' She reached into the oven and pulled out a baking tray. 'Will this do?'

'Perfect.'

Lou lined it with newspaper, tipped the litter from the litter box into it and then set it down on the sheet of newspaper outside the cage. Jake lifted the kitten out and planted him on the tray, supporting him gently. He sniffed and squatted. He yowled and made use of it immediately. 'Wow, looks like he was ready for that,' laughed Lou.

Jake lifted him out and put him back on his bed where he sat and tried again to wash himself. 'Well, that answers another question,' said Jake. 'Everything is still working properly. I'll give him a painkiller before I go.'

'Will you have a drink while you're here?'

Susie jumped up and down, pleading, 'Say yes, Dad, say yes.'

He smiled and said, 'I can't say it would go amiss, Lou. A cup of coffee would be great.'

'What would you like, Susie?'

'Could I have hot chocolate, please?'

'You certainly can. That's my favourite night-time drink too.'

Flyer purred in his bed, as if agreeing.

The house seemed very empty when they had gone and Lou was grateful for the presence of the cat. How much worse it would have been if he weren't there. She listened to the fading noise of the car engine, yawned and looked at the clock.

Time for bed.

Upstairs she drew back the curtains and opened the window, letting in fresh air. She had left Flyer downstairs tucked into his bed in the kitchen, but he had other ideas. He did not want to be by himself and his raucous yells for company soon sent her downstairs to comfort the lonely animal. Five times she went down and at last she gave up.

'It's no good, Flyer' she said. 'I can't have you on my bed in case you try and jump off in the night. We don't want you to hurt yourself even more, do we? There's nothing else for it, I'll have to move down here with you.'

She padded back upstairs to find a collection of rugs, her duvet and her pillow. These she put into the living room, making a nest for herself on the floor. She went back and fetched Flyer in his bed, laying it on the floor beside her own. 'There,' she said. 'Will that keep you happy?'

He looked up at her, his blue eyes innocent, a purr rumbling in his throat. She got into bed and reached across to turn out the side lamp. Flyer yowled softly and, in the faint light coming in from the moon, she saw him work his way up into a sitting position, crawl out of his box and make his way across her bed so that he could nestle against her.

'OK. You win,' she said. 'We might both get some sleep and at least you can't fall off.'

A small furry body tucked into her back, and his purrs resounded through the room. They became a lullaby and she slept, to wake the next morning with a paw touching her cheek and an eager little face peering into hers, telling her he needed his box and he was hungry.

She smiled and put her hand out to stroke him. Once he was fed and back in the kitchen she went upstairs to draw back the curtains. There was Janet putting bird food out in the tree in her back garden. And she could just see the roof of the house where the man called Jeff lived. Maybe she'd get to know her neighbours now she was home for good.

Twelve

Down at Twisted Willows Cottage, Jeff Grant stepped out of his back door on to the paved area, where pots of parsley, chives and marjoram flourished. Rain from last night puddled on the uneven stones and the stream was high and flooding into the lower field. Grass and rush poked up from the brown swirl of water, on which sunlight sparkled. A crow flew up from the elm tree and Jeff watched it – black against the blue of the sky. Somewhere a pheasant boomed and a sheep bleated. Life felt good.

It was the first sunny day for a week and he was looking forward to his daily walk over the fields to the shop at Woodside Farm, where he bought his eggs and milk. If he went cross-country it was only two miles, compared with five miles in the car. He liked the exercise, knew it was good for him. Otherwise, he would spend all day every day stuck at his computer writing endlessly. And he often came back with a new idea, or some problem resolved.

The Laytons treated him as a member of the family now – sitting him down in the kitchen with a mug of coffee and chatting about the business of the farm. Others came in and out too; Brad the milk tanker driver was often there, he'd seen Jake, the vet, once, and the farm workers themselves popped in and out. If it wasn't for them he would hardly talk to a soul each week.

The postman pulled up in his little red van at the side of the house and Jeff went across to take the post from him. There were only two letters and he shoved them both into his pocket to read later.

The postman grinned and said, 'Nearly got stuck in the mud, I did. I had to pull into a gateway to let another car out and it's that wet I thought I was going to be knocking at your door to give me a push!'

Jeff laughed, looking at the mud spattered across the rear wings of the van. 'I can see you did have a problem. Who was it?'

'That neighbour of yours from Brookside, Lou Barton, with a man. I think he's a policeman but he wasn't in uniform.'

Jeff frowned. 'I hope everything is OK,' he

said. He felt uncomfortable, realizing how little he knew of his neighbours – how little effort he had made to get to know them. Bits of news came his way from the postman, but he kept himself to himself.

The fields were wet after all the rain and when he arrived at Woodside Farm he squelched into the kitchen, grinning ruefully. 'I should have put my wellies on. It's like a swamp out there. I'm absolutely filthy.'

'Well, we don't mind,' said Trish, with a laugh. 'We're used to it. Now, here's your eggs and milk. Do you want anything else?'

'I'll have a look round the shop later. There are a few bits I need. I'm having a treat today to celebrate the publication of my new book and the start of the next one. It's going to be one of your lovely iced carrot cakes to go with my tea!' He smiled and patted his paunch.

Trish put a large mug of coffee in front of him and the phone rang in the next room. She bustled out, saying over her shoulder, 'Excuse me for a moment, won't you?'

He remembered the letters and pulled them both out of his pocket. One, he saw, was a statement from the bank. The other was a small, white envelope with his name and address handwritten on the front. He didn't recognize the handwriting and the postmark was blurred and illegible. He had no idea who it might be from. Fan mail for his Donko books, perhaps.

He opened it and started to read, his coffee mug in one hand.

There was a crash and Trish rushed back into the kitchen. Jeff's face was white as a sheet, his hand shaking and there was coffee everywhere.

'What on earth's the matter, Jeff? You look terrible. Here, let me clear this mess up and get you another mug.' She walked across to the sink for the dishcloth and came back to wipe the table.

Jeff pushed his chair back out of the way and said, 'Sorry. I'm sorry, Trish.'

He started to read the letter again and Trish came over with another coffee. She sat down, concern on her face and said, 'You've obviously had some bad news, Jeff. Is there anything I can do?'

He looked up and said, 'I can't take it in. I can't believe it. It's from my wife ... well, my ex-wife.'

'What does she say?' Trish asked.

He shook his head in disbelief. 'She left me for another man. Mike, his name was.

We haven't talked since she went to America with Mike and our daughter, Sandy. Now Mike's dead – killed in a car crash two years ago – and she has a brain tumour.' He paused to try and drink. His hand was still shaking so much he had to put the mug down. 'She's dying, Trish. She's come back to England and she's asking me to have our daughter to live with me.'

His voice broke and Trish patted his hand, waiting for him to recover. He wiped his eyes and said, 'I haven't seen her for six years, Trish. Six years!' He gazed into the distance, stunned by the news. Frowning, he said, 'I wish she'd told me sooner. It's so sudden. That's typical Kate.'

'Maybe she just kept hoping,' said Trish. 'She might not have known how serious it was at the beginning and then been too ill to let you know.'

'I suppose so,' said Jeff. 'It's such a shock.' The enormity of the news overwhelmed him again and he closed his eyes, trying to calm himself. The clock ticked in the silence and outside a tractor engine rumbled into life. Jeff suddenly jumped to his feet. He banged the side of his head hard with the heel of his hand and stared at Trish, his eyes wild.

'Maybe I'm dreaming. I want to wake up

and find out it's not true. Tell me I'm dreaming, Trish ... Oh God, I wished all sorts on her when she left me and even worse when she took Sandy to America and I couldn't see her. I wouldn't wish this on her though, and certainly not on poor Sandy. Oh God, Trish, it's my fault, it's my fault.' He paused and stared at her. 'Go on Trish, tell me it's not true.'

'Oh Jeff,' she replied, tears in her eyes too, 'I am so, so sorry. I wish I could. Come on. Sit down again. Let's talk about it.'

He sat down and groaned. 'How's she going to cope? How am I going to cope? I don't know her. I don't know anything about being a father. God, Trish what am I going to do?'

'You'll know,' said Trish, 'once the shock has passed. Does she say how long she has?'

'Not really. It sounds like weeks and she wants me to let her know as soon as possible about Sandy, so that she can make other plans if necessary.'

'Where would she live if you don't have her?'

'I suppose she would have to be fostered. My mother wouldn't dream of having her and there isn't anybody else.' He stopped and stared at Trish, disbelief on his face.

'What on earth am I thinking, Trish? You're right. I do know what to do. Of course I'm going to have her to live with me. I'm just not sure how good I'm going to be at it.'

'Well, none of us know that when we have children,' said Trish. 'I expect you'll muddle along like the rest of us do. And you must have been a father for a few years before your wife left.'

'That's part of the problem,' said Jeff. 'I don't think I was a very good one. I was trying to write and do a day job at the same time. It was the main reason Kate left, or so she said. "You're never here, and when you are you're in a world of your own,"were the words she used.' He stopped, seeing that last angry picture of Kate when she announced she was going – going with the man who lived down the road. A man who was there for her, she said. A man who listened to her and who had time to do things with her. *A man with a nice fat pay cheque*, Jeff had thought. A man who would buy her everything she wanted – the things she had always had and always expected to have.

He went on, 'I did spend time with Sandy though. I know I did. I used to read stories to her. Our "Donko" stories. She loved them. She gave the little dragon his name.'

Trish laughed. 'How did she come up with that?'

Jeff grinned, remembering. 'There was a donkey in the field at the bottom of our garden. We used to go and give him a carrot every evening. Sandy could never get the word "donkey" right and she called him Donko. When I began to tell her the dragon stories I wanted her to name the dragon and that's what she called him.' He paused and stared off into the distance, remembering her excitement when he liked the name. 'It was a brilliant name for him,' he said, 'because he can never decide what sort of animal he is! I've always written the stories for her, and dedicated each new book to her.'

Sighing, he said, 'I don't know if Kate bought them for her though. I never heard from her. That's what bothers me. Perhaps Kate painted a really black picture of me and Sandy doesn't really want to know me. What if she hates me, Trish?'

'I doubt she does,' said Trish. 'It'll sort. These things do. It won't be easy for you but you know you can ask us for help, or talk to us. And you'll bring her to meet us, won't you? I'm so glad you found out here and not by yourself at home. That would have been even worse.'

Jeff managed another grin and said, 'I have to agree with you there. Thanks, Trish. And of course I'll bring Sandy over. Anyway, I'd better go. I need to phone Kate and let her know.'

Jeff had inherited the farmhouse in its little patch of land from his godmother, much to his surprise and delight. He thought at first that he would sell it and use the money to buy somewhere else in town; a new beginning that didn't have reminders of his life with Kate.

But then he'd lost his job.

He'd known it was coming.

Too many nights when he had sought solace in the pub; too many mornings when he had been late for work; too many mornings arriving unkempt, unwashed and still smelling of the night before. He'd known it couldn't go on and his dismissal had made him sort himself out.

He'd decided to move to The Twisted Willows, leave behind his old life and begin a new career as a writer – a serious writer.

His mother, of course, was horrified.

His job was part of her status. A sales director was something to boast about, something to say with your head held high. It implied smart cars, smart houses and smart families. The divorce had been bad enough. Except she had found a way to present it so that it sounded as if poor Kate had been unable to deal with the pressures that went with her husband's high-powered executive job and had left for a more mundane lifestyle. She chose to ignore the fact that he was a small cog in a big wheel.

A writer though! Even worse, a writer of children's books! Where was the kudos in that?

He had always wanted to write – loving the power of words when he was at school, of making stories from his imagination come alive on the page. But writing was not a career aspiration and teachers and his mother had made him abandon the idea. He vividly remembered the horror on their faces when he had said what he wanted to do. It made him wonder why they'd bothered asking. Like there was a tick list of ten acceptable jobs, and any other path was to be scorned.

He decided to make it his priority, his number one priority. Now there were six Donko books in the series and another one about to be published. He was looking forward to starting the next one, and wanted to write a book for adults too.

The house groaned with furniture. He had brought some of his and kept most of his godmother's. It was old, heavy and too large for the rooms but it served its purpose. Then there were the boxes: piles of cardboard boxes in the two bedrooms he didn't use. Boxes containing his old life that he hadn't wanted to think about, to deal with. They would have to go. He couldn't expect his daughter to settle into a house that he had still not managed to make into a home for himself.

Going through a box full of papers – old bills, bank statements, letters – he found drawings that Sandy had done. There was a crooked house with smoke pouring from its chimney and a bright yellow sun beaming down from a blue sky. Here were little stick men and strange animals. Then, a picture of Mummy and Daddy and her, all holding hands.

What had she thought when her life had been turned upside down?

He came across a poem he had written after Kate left. It brought the time back into sharp focus. There, in the first line, was the question, 'Was there love once?' How long ago it seemed since he had written it. In the first months after her departure his rage had been all-consuming. He had still seen Sandy every week but the visits had been tarnished by the anger he felt. In the end Kate had been unable to bear it and, when Mike was offered a job in America, he took it – and Kate and Sandy too. It was then that Jeff had made a conscious decision to freeze all feeling.

The poem held images of snow, of December lasting forever.

He'd told himself he didn't care, and that Sandy was better off without him: no contact was better than limited contact. How could he afford to go over to America, especially after he'd lost his job? That part of his life was over. His contact with Sandy had been reduced to the Donko books. He wrote them for her, for the four-year-old daughter he had once had. All the books were dedicated to her – 'to my darling daughter' – so that, if Kate bought them for her, Sandy would know that he hadn't forgotten her. He hadn't even known where they lived. Kate had sent him an address but he had burnt it. When regret hit he reminded himself that he had decided – he had frozen out that part of his life. He didn't know that Sandy had written to him – her letters going to his old address.

He crumpled the poem up and threw it in the bin.

There was a photograph of Sandy. It was almost the last time he had seen her. She was feeding a carrot to the donkey she called Donko and grinning back at him. He hadn't been able to bear seeing it before. Now he took it out and stared at it.

What would she look like? In the photo she was four years old. Now she was ten. Would he even recognize her? Her hair was dark, straight and cut into a bob. It framed her face, pink from the cold air, and that cheeky grin. She wore a duffel coat – bright blue with wooden toggles to fasten it – which she called her Paddington coat; pink wellies were on her feet. He wiped the surface of the photo frame with his cuff and placed it carefully on the mantelpiece. She would know he hadn't forgotten her, and perhaps it would help him to believe what was happening.

Whilst tidying, he realized he wouldn't be able to do it all before she arrived. There were only two weeks and a room for her was what was needed most. First though, he finished sorting the boxes and had a huge bonfire in the back garden, burning the clutter of his past.

Smoke drifted on the wind and into next door where Janet was hanging washing on the line. She frowned and changed her mind, wondering what was going on. She had never known him have a bonfire before.

A van came to take some of the furniture. The wallpaper was faded, old and dropping off in places. He gathered his energy and spent a day pulling it all off. Underneath, the plaster was reasonable and he decided to emulsion it. Would she still like pink? Perhaps not. He decided to go for a bright yellow instead – the colour of sunshine and hope.

He decorated the walls with the illustrations from the publishers. At the head of her bed was Donko, trying to get into the pouch of an enraged kangaroo. On the opposite wall Donko followed behind a line of fluffy, yellow ducklings who were about to jump into the pond after their mother. In a third one, there was Donko on a green hillside rounding up a flock of sheep. The sheepdog snapped at his tail and the shepherd stood on the hilltop waving his crook angrily and shouting at the little dragon. The illustrator had captured the spirit of the stories perfectly.

He thought of the new book. There was a deadline to meet and he hadn't been able to think straight since last week. Ideas had deserted him. His editor was complaining that they were going to be short of time. His usual problem was thinking of a satisfactory ending. Now he couldn't even think of a satisfactory beginning.

He hoped Sandy would like her room. There would be time to change things together – new bedding and curtains, and a different colour on the walls perhaps. At least it looked inviting now, even if it was old-fashioned. But the furniture suited the cottage: an old washstand, a walnut wardobe with a mirror in one door, an old, white, painted bookcase with the Donko books resting on the top shelf. She could look out of the window on to the stream and the fields, see the cows and watch the birds.

He sighed and yawned. He hadn't been able to sleep since he heard the news – his thoughts a riot of things he would have to think about when Sandy was here with him. He shied away from thinking about the big issues: the death of her mother that she knew was coming, and living with a father she hadn't seen or heard from for years.

He took refuge in thinking about the little things that went to make up the days. There was school to think about, as well as clothes, inoculations, friends, and what she liked to eat. He tossed restlessly, worrying endlessly.

He was used to following his own routine – the walk to the farm shop, the days spent writing, the evenings with a book or TV, listening to music. For both of them, they would have to reinvent a life together.

Thirteen

On the day of Kate and Sandy's arrival Jeff stood at the window, looking out at the farmland around him. The pheasant called its warning. He thought back to that last day, almost a fortnight ago now, on which he had known peace of mind, when life was feeling good. He should have known. Fate did not work like that. He wished he knew the other people who lived on the lane, but even if he did, they couldn't be much help. There were no other children.

He had asked Kate if he should come to collect Sandy.

No, was the answer; someone would bring them and Kate wanted to know what sort of home he had. The cottage hadn't been a place she ever visited; she had met his godmother only in London, when she'd taken them out for a meal. Kate hadn't known of his move, so when Sandy hadn't got replies to her letters Kate had thought he didn't care. It was only the dedications in his books, which she had still bought, that had given her the courage to contact him.

Jeff had coffee percolating and had arranged a plate of Bourbon biscuits. Surely any child would like those? There was orange squash for Sandy.

Kate had said they would arrive at eleven. It was only a few minutes past when the car drew up at the gate. Jeff braced himself. Their last contact had been horrible, he remembered. An angry exchange of criticisms and hurt, which had ended in Kate marching off, holding Sandy's hand. Sandy had been sobbing and he had wanted to run after her and pull her to him. Let Kate go to America by herself, he had thought. What right did she have to take his child away? He hadn't been able to do it though, knowing that it was already unbearable for his small daughter.

At first he thought that this was another car, containing three strangers. A young woman was driving, and there was an older woman beside her. The driver came round to help her companion and Jeff was shocked, realizing that this was Kate. She was so thin – her face gaunt and her eyes enormous under a head-hugging crocheted hat, which was grey with a bright-blue flower stitched to one side.

It was the only thing that was familiar. Kate had always loved hats.

She needed help to get out of the car and walk towards him. He became aware of the girl who followed her and stood, uncertain, one foot scratching the back of her other leg. She was slim and suntanned, her long, dark hair was pulled into a ponytail, and she was wearing jeans and a red tee shirt.

He stood, feeling helpless and horrified. Words deserted him.

'I've coffee ready,' he said at last, taking refuge in hospitality. 'We could have it in the garden.'

'I'd rather not stay ... it would be too painful,' Kate said. Her eyes were bright with tears and Jeff wanted to take hold of her and wipe them away. He realized his anger had burnt out long ago and all he felt now was an overwhelming sadness for her. The love he had first felt for her was still there – a gentler love though, that understood her for what she was and for what she was going through. He put out his hand towards her and she took it, looking up at him with her pain-filled eyes.

'Better to say goodbye fast. For both of us. Sandy knows what's happening.' She turned to look down at the child, and held out her other hand. The girl took it and stood beside her, leaning against her mother, her eyes cast down as if she could not bear to see her father.

'Sandy, this is your dad,' said Kate.

'Hi, Sandy,' Jeff said. It was a feeble response but words had left him again. The years of silence felt insurmountable. He stood still, knowing that any embrace would be unwelcome.

Sandy looked up at him as he spoke. He saw his own eyes, but she had her mother's colouring. He wondered what she was thinking. 'Would you like to look round the cottage with us and see Sandy's room?' he asked Kate.

'Yes, I so want to be able to imagine her

here,' Kate said. Even her voice was different, as if every word was an effort. There was no strength in her. She turned to her companion. 'This is Beth. She's from the hospice.'

Jeff shook the proffered hand.

It took some minutes to negotiate the drive. Beth supported Kate on one side and Jeff kept hold of her arm, grateful that she accepted his touch. Sandy walked quietly behind them. Kate peeped in at the kitchen, the living room and the room that Jeff used as a study. There, Beth lowered her into an armchair and she struggled for breath. She said, 'There's no way I can get up the stairs. Sandy, you go with your dad and look at your room. You can tell me all about it.'

Jeff sensed that the child was unwilling to leave her mother, but she followed him up the stairs and into the room he had prepared for her. 'We can get new curtains and covers if you don't like these,' he said, hoping that the offer would help her feel some ownership. 'And new pictures. I expect these are a bit young for you.'

Sandy looked about her, and then smiled. It was only a momentary gesture, but it gave Jeff hope that this might be easier than he had feared. 'Donko!' she said. 'I love him. I always did. Mum bought me all the new books and I always checked the front page to make sure you had remembered to dedicate it to me. That's why I wrote to you.' She stopped and wiped a tear furiously from her cheek. 'Why didn't you answer?' she asked quietly.

Jeff sat down on the bed and patted the cover beside him. 'Sit down, Sandy,' he said. He could hardly speak for the tightness in his throat. Tears that he had never wept were surfacing and it was all he could do to keep them in check. He put his arm round her shoulders and stroked her hair. 'I never got them,' he said, 'because I moved here when I lost my job after you'd gone. And I didn't have an address to get in touch with you, because I burnt it. I was so angry.'

He felt ashamed – ashamed that someone he loved so much should have been hurt by his own unmanaged pain. 'I am so sorry, Sandy,' he said.

His daughter leant against him for a moment, and turned her head to look at him. 'Don't cry, Daddy.' she said. She opened her case and pulled something out from the top. 'Look, I've got a donkey called Donko! Could I have a real donkey, do you think? Then we could feed him carrots like we did before?'

So she had remembered.

'We'll start looking for one tomorrow,' Jeff said with a grin. It should be easy to find a donkey, he thought. The farmer might rent him a bit of paddock. Jeff knew he would have agreed to an elephant if it would make Sandy feel better.

'It's a lovely room,' she told her mother, once they were back downstairs. 'Lots of pictures of Donko. And we're going to get a donkey. And I can choose new curtains and bedcovers. I think I'd like pale green ones. They would look nice with the yellow walls.'

'I'm glad you like it, darling,' her mother said. Jeff guessed that tears were not far away.

Beth put a hand under her arm. 'Maybe we'd better go,' she said.

No use prolonging the agony.

Kate hugged her daughter. 'Be good for daddy,' she said. 'Write me lots of letters, won't you, love?'

'Every day,' Sandy promised.

Jeff moved over and hugged Kate gently. She leaned against his chest and he bent to kiss her cheek. 'I'll look after her, Kate,' he whispered. 'I promise ... try not to worry about her.'

Kate gently removed his hands and kissed one of them before she let it go. Beth helped her into the car and they drove away. Kate didn't look back.

Sandy watched the car drive away. She stood at the gate for a long time, as if that might bring her mother back to her. Jeff longed to hug her again, but knew she must come to that in her own time. He couldn't imagine what she was feeling. She must think her whole life was in ruins.

'Come and have some orange squash, Sandy,' he said. 'I need a cup of coffee. Then we must unpack your cases. Tomorrow you can come with me when I go to the farm for milk and eggs. They might know where we can buy a donkey. Would you like that?'

Sandy nodded. She looked up at him with tear-filled eyes. He had expected sobs, but he expected she had had a lot of practice at hiding her feelings. Life wasn't fair, Jeff thought, savage with anger at the cruel blow that had been dealt out to a small girl who should have been enjoying her childhood and instead was facing up to a situation that daunted adults.

And she had already suffered when her stepfather died. Had she loved Mike?

Jeff unpacked the cases for her. She put

the clothes away in the drawers, and put her toys around the room. There was Donko – battered and much loved. She put him on her bed. There was not much in the way of property. He looked at the books. All the Donko stories, and others by authors he did not know, except for *The Wind in The Willows* and the *Pooh* books; *The Box of Delights* and *The Narnia Chronicles*.

He found an envelope that Kate had left in the study when he was upstairs with Sandy. He opened it that night after Sandy had gone reluctantly to her bed.

'Hug?' he'd asked, looking down at the forlorn little face.

She nodded and he sat beside her and held her in his arms. The tears came and when the storm subsided he kissed her and straightened the covers.

'You won't die too?' she asked. 'Mike died. In a car crash. When I was seven. Everybody goes away. And when you never wrote to me I was afraid you had stopped loving me, even if you did still dedicate the books to me.'

Tears welled and he bent to kiss her on her forehead. He looked down at her. 'It's so hard to explain,' he said. 'It's like wanting something so much and knowing you can't have it, so you pretend it's not there, not something you want, because it's the only way you can bear it.'

Sandy looked up at him. 'I suppose it's like me pretending that Mum's not going to die. I don't want her to so I pretend that she isn't. You won't leave me again, will you?'

'I hope I won't leave you,' Jeff said. He could think of nothing to console her. 'Would you like me to read you a Donko story? We must find you some more grown-up books tomorrow.'

'Please. The first one, where he thinks he's a duck. I used to look at the pictures and pretend that you were reading to me. That was the only one then.'

She fell asleep before he had got to the end. He left the landing light on and her door open, lest she wake.

Kate's letter contained only lists of things that Sandy needed, of her likes and dislikes with food, and her birth certificate and christening record card.

Jeff sat downstairs in the dark, long into the night, wondering how on earth he was going to cope.

Fourteen

How lovely it was, Lou thought, looking out of the living room window at heavy rain yet again, to be able to stay at home. The stream had flooded into the bottom half of Brookside's sloping land and was lapping at the boundary fence that separated field from garden. Autumn was well on the way; sodden leaves from the fruit trees littered the grass, and a few apples were still clinging to bare branches. With the heavy curtains between living room and dining room drawn across, firelight flickering, the room was a haven of warmth.

Lou put down her battered copy of the *Just So Stories*, leaned back and stretched. Disturbed by the movement, Flyer opened one blue eye and yowled softly. He tucked his nose back into the curl of his body, purring in response to the soft touch of Lou's hand. She laughed, remembering the story she had just been reading – 'The Cat that Walked by Himself'.

'You wouldn't know how to be aloof, would you?' she said to Flyer.

He purred more loudly and Lou wished her mother were still around so that she could meet him. It was her mother who'd used to read the *Just So Stories* to her when she was small. Never having been around cats before, Lou realized that that was how she had believed they all behaved.

Aloof and condescending, needing nobody.

Flyer clearly had different ideas!

Lou had to laugh at herself. *I still think like I did when I was five*, she thought now, remembering standing under the buddleia bush in the garden. Drooping spikes of deep-purple flowers hanging above her head, and multicoloured butterflies fluttering and perching to sip the nectar. Lou had watched intently for ages, and then gone inside to say sadly to her mother, 'They must all be in a good temper, Mum. None of the butterflies have stamped.' How her mother had laughed!

Looking round her living room, Lou wished that she, too, could have purred with contentment. It was eight weeks since Flyer had come to live with her.

Eight weeks ago it had been little more

than a waiting room.

A place in which the past echoed.

Now it told a different story, resonating with the announcement, 'Flyer lives here!'

There lay the hearth rug, pulled askew because he had been trying to kill it – grabbing at the corner with his front paws, kicking at the fringed edge with his back legs, biting and swearing low in his throat. The tail of a catnip mouse dangled limply from under a settee cushion where Susie had hidden it; another lay in her discarded slipper. Crumpled paper balls littered the floor and one dangled from the doorknob on a length of string. A shredded sheet of newspaper lay like confetti beside Lou's chair and the rest of it made a tunnel on the floor.

On the mantelpiece a framed photograph of Flyer stood beside Johnny's. A tray holding three empty mugs, a glass and a plate, on which all that was left were biscuit crumbs, rested on the coffee table.

Lou thought back over the last two months. It had been quite a journey for both of them.

'How are you both getting on?' Jake had asked on the second day, when he and Susie returned in the evening.

For answer, Lou took them into the living

room.

Jake raised one eyebrow when he saw the tumbled bedding. 'Sleeping on the floor, Lou?'

'It says it all,' she told him, a rueful expression on her face. 'He demands and I obey!'

Jake grinned and said, 'And to think that I dared to suggest you might not look after him properly. What happened?'

'He made it clear, in no uncertain terms, that he was not going to be left alone in the kitchen at night, however many times I told him how nice his bed was. I must have tried five times to get him settled. I gave up in the end and decided to sleep down here. I didn't want to take him up on to my bed in case he decided to jump off in the night.' She waved an arm at the bedding. 'So here we sleep. Even now he still insists on crawling out of his own bed and sleeping as close to me as he can get!'

Jake had laughed, saying, 'He's a character, this one. There's no doubt about it. He certainly loves people.'

That first week, when Flyer and Lou had been learning about each other, he had been able to do little more than talk to her. He had something to say about everything; the inflections of his voice were full of information about what he thought of his new world. No cat she had ever known had a voice like his. A voice that could be raised to a pitch that brooked no denying. A voice with so many variations it was easy to believe he was eagerly telling her all about what he thought of the world. She often found herself joining in the conversation with him.

Johnny laughed at her from the mantelpiece and she laughed back. 'Yes, Johnny,' she said. 'I have gone quite mad.'

And Flyer said, 'Waugh!' in agreement.

After three nights of sleeping downstairs she and Jake decided that he was so anxious for her company that there was no way he was going to try and get off the bed in the middle of the night. 'Joined at the hip, I think,' said Jake.

Lou looked at him, enjoying the transformation of his face when he smiled. Grief, stress and tiredness had soured his expression to a habitual frown of worry. Those fleeting moments when he relaxed showed a different man – a man with a sense of humour and a love for the silliness of life.

The idea of keeping Flyer in confinement had had to be abandoned too. His indignation at being shut in had been exhausting for both of them. In the end Lou gave in. Flyer crept out, just managing to bear his own weight on his back legs and collapsed sideways on to the floor with a pathetic cry.

Lou phoned Jake and said, 'I don't know what to do for the best.'

'Don't worry,' he said. 'As long as you keep an eye on him so that he doesn't walk too much he should be fine. It's more important that he doesn't try to jump off anything.'

Lou looked down at the little animal. He gazed up at her, blue eyes wide.

'OK, you win,' she said. She took his fleece sleeping blanket out of the cage, tucked it into the cardboard box she had first used to take him to the vet, and then carefully lifted him and placed him on it. 'There you are. I'll carry you round as though you were a god!' she said, folding her hands and bowing.

He purred.

The days developed a routine, dictated by Flyer. She imagined it must be a bit like having a new baby in the house. Her time was no longer her own because Flyer insisted he share every moment of it. While he was unable to move, she delighted in spending the whole day with him. Fire blazing, a supply of books and magazines, and music in the background – it was heaven!

He lay on his bed and purred whilst she stroked him, careful to avoid his sore places. Her touch was soothing and slowly the young cat relaxed, accepting his new owner and his new home. Here was food and comfort; warmth and company. He wanted only to be near her, to see and smell her, and to feel her hands upon him.

Every morning she was awoken by his paw tapping her face gently, his rough tongue licking her cheek. She'd greet him, stroking his head, lying drowsy and warm, not wanting to move. He'd yowl, reminding her that he was hungry and wanted his breakfast. If she didn't move quickly enough his demands would become more insistent until she relented, pushed back the duvet and climbed sleepily out of bed. She'd scoop him up and carefully lay him in his box to carry him into the bathroom with her. He'd watch her, eyes wide with astonishment at the noise of running water, ears twitching.

Downstairs again, she'd prepare his breakfast. Always a tasty plate of fish mixed with rice. Once he was eating, Lou prepared her own breakfast and ate whilst Flyer washed his face and attempted to wash the rest of himself too. At first he could only manage a few licks round his hindquarters before he collapsed, so most of his washing was done whilst he lay on his side. The effort wore him out and he would sleep. Lou seized these moments to catch up with jobs until an indignant yell from the kitchen announced he was awake and where was she?

Even though she had felt lonely when she worked away from home, she missed people and was glad of the daily visits made by Jake and Susie. Ray, too, was a frequent visitor, eager to see how the young cat was progressing.

Towards the end of the first week she had carefully shut Flyer in his cage and told him she had to go shopping. His protests had started as soon as she closed the door; indignant shouts assaulted her ears. She had got as far as the front door before giving up, afraid he might damage himself with his distress. That evening she asked Ray if he would mind getting some shopping for her.

'He's a bit of a tyrant, that one, isn't he?' said Ray, when Lou explained what had happened.

'I don't mind,' said Lou. 'I expect it's because everything is new and he's afraid of being alone. Those hours on the road must have been dreadful.'

Ray teased her, 'You're a soft one, aren't you?' and Lou laughed and agreed.

Inside, she thought that the cat needed someone to be soft with him – more than anything else in the world. She had begun to wonder about Ray, interested in getting to know him better, but she decided then that perhaps he wasn't quite what she wanted – or needed.

Gradually Flyer's strength returned and he began to walk a little.

'He seems to think he's a retriever,' Lou said one day when Jake and Susie called. It was the fourth week of Flyer's arrival in her life. Ray had turned up earlier in the afternoon and was ensconced in the armchair with a mug of coffee. 'He spends a lot of the day trying to walk. He takes long rests between. He loves to carry small things and leaves them all over the place.'

'He used to do three steps and then a lie down,' Susie said. 'Then four steps and a lie down.'

Lou nodded in agreement and said, 'He did that about ten times, three or four times a day. He's black determined and if he can't do things one way he'll work out another.

He's incredible.'

'He does better than humans,' Ray said. 'Anyone would think he'd consulted a physiotherapist!'

Lou laughed, with a vision of the little cat sitting solemnly in front of the therapist and listening intently.

At the end of each day he waited at the foot of the stairs to be taken up for bed. In between, he intended to get around in spite of his injury and explored wherever he could.

But he wanted an audience whilst he did it.

If it wasn't to tell her what he was doing and what he thought about it, it was to demand that she tell him how clever he was. If she left him in the living room he managed to reach the kitchen, though his progress was slow. As his strength returned he always managed to follow her.

Ray had put business cards out for her and there were some at Jake's practice too. The number of clients she had was growing as word got about. Sometimes new ones came to the house and then Flyer was sure they had come especially to see him. He rubbed against their legs and purred loudly, and then sat and looked at them when they sat down. He longed to try out their laps but jumping was still beyond him.

Whenever Lou sat down at her computer he was there, demanding her attention. He hated her to sit at the desk – hated her watching the screen and not him. He sat on the floor by her chair and cried pitifully. Clearing a space for him, she fetched a rug from upstairs and put it on the desk. She picked him up and put him on it. His tail twitched with excitement.

A new territory to explore!

He patted at the cables, sniffed round the screen, stared at the moving images of the screen saver and tried to catch one of the fish that swam across it. He sat on the keyboard and wrote his own epic.

She plucked him off and put him down on the rug saying, 'There, Flyer, that's yours. Now stay there, please! Otherwise we won't be able to eat and you know you wouldn't like that!'

She worked to the rumble of his purr.

The stairs defeated him and he hated it when she went up without him. It was impossible to ignore his yowls. When she needed to go upstairs she carried him up with her. So long as he could see her, he did not complain.

As the bones healed he was able to explore more, finding little recesses where he could hide – places where he felt safe if there were strange noises outside. There was an RAF airbase near, and sometimes jets flew screaming over the house. Flyer could not bear the noise and even if Lou were there he panicked and hid.

One dreadful morning she couldn't find him anywhere and convinced herself he had managed to get out.

It was the lack of noise that was so strange.

She hadn't thought to look upstairs, thinking the stairs were beyond him. But he had managed it that day and she finally unearthed him from the airing cupboard where she had put some ironing to air earlier. There he was, curled up on a fleece-covered hot water bottle beside the hot-water tank, sound asleep after his exertions. He woke and greeted her.

'Clever boy,' Lou said. 'I knew you could climb one stair but not all of them.'

Jake and Susie arrived one day to find Lou standing at the sink bathing scratches on both arms. Flyer crouched on his bed by the cooker. His ears were back, a low growl rumbled in his throat and his tail was bushed. Susie bent to stroke him and he swore loudly at her.

She stood up in alarm, saying, 'What's the matter with him?'

Lou said, 'I thought it would be a good idea to take him outside to look round the garden and get some fresh air. He's not been outside for ages. We got down the bottom to where the apple trees are and a crow flew overhead. He took one look at it, shrieked and then tried to jump from my arms. I didn't want him to and got these for my pains. We had quite a tussle before I got back inside with him.' She paused to mop at a bleeding scratch and said, 'I feel awful. Poor little mite.'

'Here, let me do that for you,' said Jake. 'It is my job after all.'

Lou laughed and handed him the cotton wool and Susie sat down on the floor by Flyer's bed. His fur had begun to settle and he let Susie stroke him.

Jake mopped the trickle of blood from Lou's arm. He said, 'It might take him a while to get used to the big outdoors again. He obviously still remembers the bird taking him. You'll just have to be patient and wait to see if his curiosity gets the better of him.'

'I hope he does. I know he'll have a lovely

time out there. Maybe I should get a pram to push him in!'

Susie giggled and said, 'Dressed in a little bonnet and shawl!'

'I've got a better idea,' said Jake, his eyes twinkling. 'One with a bit more dignity...'

'What?' asked Lou, intrigued.

'Aha! Wait and see,' said Jake.

They sat, drinking coffee and watching Susie playing with Flyer. She was pretending to throw a ping-pong ball and then hiding it.

But he always knew where it was – his blue eyes intent on her every movement.

Lou watched him and said, 'I never realized how clever animals can be!'

Jake chuckled. 'Much cleverer than we are,' he said. 'I can't tell you how many times I've been fooled by a dog or a cat, or even a cow or a sheep. One of my patients is a menace. He's a big German Shepherd and there is no door that has ever defied him. All the doors now have bolts at the top. He hasn't yet worked out a way of dealing with those. There's a padlock on the refrigerator too. He learned that if he put his paw in the crack he could open it. He's one of the cleverest I've met.'

Lou quickly put her hands over Flyer's

ears and laughed. 'Don't let him hear you saying that! He sits and worships the fridge in case the door opens by itself!'

Susie looked up, her eyes alight with amusement, and said, 'And then there was the dog foxhound that got into the bitch side of the Hunt kennels. Do you remember, Dad?'

Jake looked at his daughter. She was a different child when she was away from the surgery and home. She had a quirky view of the world and Lou responded to it, obviously finding her refreshing. Jake was remembering. 'I'd forgotten about him, Susie. That was another instance of an animal working out something totally unexpected,' he said to Lou. 'The huntsman was on holiday and he asked a friend to look after the hounds. He was mystified each morning to find one of the dogs in with the bitches. Luckily none of them was in season.'

'Did they find out how he did it?' Lou asked.

'The man stayed one night and hid. As soon as it was dark the dog got into the trough, submerged, and crawled to the other side of the wall and then got out again. None of the others ever followed him and nobody knew how he had worked out the way to achieve his goal. The trough was blocked off after that and he was foiled.'

'You're joking,' Lou said, unable to believe the story.

'He's not,' Susie said. 'I was there when Bob told us what had happened. Dad suggested putting in a barrier to stop him. So they did and spoiled his fun...'

Even now Flyer no longer needed attention it had stayed as a habit that Jake and Susie looked in two or three times a week. Sometimes Jake left her while he went back to evening surgery or to do a visit. The time always seemed to pass quickly – playing, chatting, watching TV and doing homework.

In truth they were both glad to be away from the surgery. Susie herself felt happier when she was with Lou and Jake was just pleased to have some peace and quiet.

'How is the new receptionist?' Lou asked one night.

Jake groaned and said, 'Don't ask.'

'Why not? Isn't she doing the job well?'

'Oh, yes, she is. But I don't know what's got into Alison. I thought she would be pleased for the extra help. God knows, she's had to put in a lot of extra work in the past year. But she's driving me mad with her constant questions and she and Christine seem to be always bickering at each other.'

Susie looked up, a length of string dangling from one hand. 'It's because she fancies you, Dad. She's afraid that you might fancy Christine so she's making sure you notice her – how much *she* does, how much *she* cares.'

Flyer pounced on the end of the string and Susie trailed it across the floor and under a corner of newspaper. He lay down and tried to fish it out from underneath.

Jake snorted. 'You've been reading too many teen magazines, Susie. Of course she doesn't fancy me. I'm about fifteen years older than her, which is nearly old enough to be her father.'

'Hmm,' said Lou. 'That doesn't stop her fancying you. Susie might be right.'

'Life,' he commented bitterly, 'would be so much easier without people. You know where you are with animals.'

As if to prove him right, Flyer left his game with Susie and struggled up on to his lap where he snuggled down and butted with his head against Jake's hand, demanding to be stroked and purring loudly.

Lou laughed. 'He often does that,' she

said. 'He seems to know when I need comforting!'

'Lou, talking of fancying,' Jake said. 'What about this policeman that keeps coming round. Do you think he fancies you?' He couldn't believe he had asked the question, but he knew he really wanted to know the answer. There was something about Lou. Her company warmed him in a way that he hadn't felt for a long time. Ever since they had finally had to accept Eileen was dying he had felt lost, as though it wasn't his real life he was living any more. Now he began to feel as if he were coming home from a long journey in a strange land.

Lou looked embarrassed. 'He did, a bit, I think. He asked me to go out with him several times and, in the end, I had to tell him I wasn't interested. He's a nice man but he's too young for me and, to be honest, I'm not ready for anything except friendship at the moment.' She glanced over at the photograph on the mantelpiece and added, 'It still feels too soon and Johnny is still too real to me.'

Jake nodded. 'I know what you mean. I feel like that about my wife. I can't imagine being with anybody else. Was he all right about it?'

'Oh, yes. He still calls in because he likes to see how Flyer is. I don't mind. I like him and it would be good to see him happy with someone else. I needn't feel guilty about rejecting him, then! He said something about "Young Farmers" so I think he's hoping to find a new girlfriend there!'

Flyer still refused to leave the house. Outdoors terrified him.

Jake arrived late one morning with a light lead and a small harness. Lou looked at it and said, 'Aha! That was what you were talking about, was it? A lead, instead of a pram!'

'I hope so,' said Jake. 'You can take him outside for short walks. It'll help to get his strength back and he might get used to being outside, and feel more confident when he has you with him. Then make the walks longer each day. It'll bring back his muscle condition too.'

Flyer hated the harness, which Lou put on him so that he could get used to it before she attached the lead. He sat and scratched furiously, trying to dislodge it. It was nearly five days before he accepted it, and then the lead was something to be chased and pounced on – certainly not something for the purpose for which it was intended.

'Put it on him and let him drag it around,' Jake suggested. 'Then pick it up and follow him. Don't try to influence him.'

It was easier said than done, but Lou did not give up. Their first expedition was down the drive, with Flyer trying to keep under the bushes where he would be unseen from the sky. It was a difficult journey for both of them.

Gradually, they went further.

Janet, watching from behind her curtain, was horrified. Whoever heard of a cat being walked on a lead? She began to doubt Lou's sanity. It was utterly ridiculous, but maybe it was better than having him wander freely, able to trespass where he chose.

Lou and Flyer passed Janet's gate daily. He preferred to go down the lane rather than into the back garden, lured by familiar smells from the derelict Lane End Farm.

Janet watched in despair, feeling even more of a prisoner in her own house. How could she go out? She might meet them on her way home. She tried to find some system in Lou's walks, but Lou, no longer timed by working hours, went out whenever the mood took her, or when she felt that Flyer was getting restive and could do with a change of scene.

At last he did not mind walking beside her on the lead outside. No bird would descend while he was with Lou. They walked a little further each day. When he was tired he lay down and rested. Lou tried leaving the back door open so he could go out by himself. He sat and looked, but as soon as he saw a bird he would dash back to the safety of his bed.

'He'll never forget,' Jake said. 'He'll probably feel an urge to explore, but he's always going to be cautious. All the same it might be an idea to snip him ... the call of a she cat may override his caution and anyway, I don't suppose you want him spraying in the house.'

Lou grimaced and said, 'Not particularly. But there aren't any cats near for him to be tempted by.'

Jake laughed. 'The scent comes on the wind. They can catch it from miles away, believe me. Many an owner has felt her cat was safe, but then they come to me in dismay with a litter on the way. And cats are fertile very young. They have kittens at six months.'

Lou thought Flyer might be upset at going back to the surgery, but he greeted everyone as if they were old friends. He did not seem unduly distressed when she collected him, finding him not in his cage but in Susie's arms.

Back home he inspected every inch of his territory, as if wondering if some intruder had been there in his absence. Satisfied, and somewhat sore, he settled on Lou's lap, in spite of the fact that she was seated at her computer, trying to make sense of a particularly messy set of accounts.

He recovered fast and not only resumed his daily walks, but, after a few weeks, began to venture further into the garden, though never far from the house and only if the door was left open so that he could dive to safety inside. He had no desire to go unless Lou was near.

Fifteen

Janet tore open Frances' letter eagerly. They had met up a couple of times since that first encounter and had written to each other too. On Monday Frances should be here to go shopping with her. The thought of going down the lane in the car was wonderful. No risk of encountering that awful cat. She started to read then put the letter down, disappointment overwhelming her. Frances couldn't make it after all.

She started reading again, feeling irritated because Frances told her off for not going out and suggested she just get on with it! That it was silly to be put off by a cat! She knew she should heed the advice and it was kindly meant. She scolded herself, saying, 'Pull yourself together, Janet, and just do it.'

She knew she simply had to. Once again, she was running out of food. Maybe she should give up eating! Sighing, she looked at the clock and realized that the bus went in twenty minutes. She would have to get ready and go.

When she returned from her enforced expedition on the bus to the supermarket in Larksbridge she was laden with shopping bags. They were heavy – cutting into her gloved hands and numbing them. Her breath steamed in the cold air and she longed for her fire and a hot drink. She set the bags down part way along the track and leaned against a gate. It wasn't much further but it seemed like miles. The grey horse that lived in the field came up behind her and huffed. She turned and patted his neck.

'Hello, Captain,' she said. 'Would you like a carrot?' She rummaged in the bags and took one out, offering it to him on the palm of her hand. His soft mouth nuzzled and picked it up. She patted him again as he crunched, and thought how ridiculous she was. Unafraid of a great big horse and terrified of a small, furry cat.

She picked up the bags and set off, rounding the bend that brought her to the front of Lou's house. To her horror, Lou was coming up the lane with Flyer on the lead. Janet stopped in her tracks, her heart pounding and her skin suddenly clammy.

Lou called to her, 'Do you need a hand with those bags?' and walked towards her.

Janet couldn't answer. Panic struck. Her legs felt as if they would not carry her, her heart raced, and she was sure she would collapse. 'Please,' Janet begged, her voice trembling, 'take him away. Don't let him near me. Take him away. Please.'

Lou was startled. She was afraid her neighbour might have a heart attack. She looked dreadful. Surely, it wasn't the sight of the cat? 'I'll put him indoors and come back and carry those for you,' she said. 'Don't move. I promise I won't bring him closer.'

She put Flyer inside, who was protesting loudly because his walk had been cut short. She removed the lead and then ran back to Janet, who still seemed unable to move. Lou looked at her white face, really concerned.

She picked up the bags, and led the way to Janet's cottage. Janet produced her key but her hands were trembling so much she couldn't put it in the door. Lou took it from her, opened the door and led her inside.

'Sit and rest. Can I make you a cup of tea? Ought I to send for your doctor?'

'No, I'm not ill. I don't need a doctor,' Janet gasped. 'I'll be fine in a few minutes. It's just ... I've always been afraid of cats. My mother hated them.' She stopped again, trying to catch her breath. 'She was sure I'd get scratched and die of cat scratch fever, or some other horrible disease that they cause. Every time a cat came anywhere near she would start screaming and rush me inside.'

'Well, I've never heard of anyone catching anything from a cat,' Lou said, hoping it would comfort Janet.

Janet told her, 'There's a tray already laid in the kitchen, if you can spare the time to make tea. All you need to do is boil the kettle, if you don't mind.'

'Of course not,' said Lou as she went out into the kitchen. It was old-fashioned, and retained the charm of a bygone age. An old pine dresser, resplendent with a fine display of willow pattern plates, dominated one wall. Her grandmother had had some just like those. And there were two dishes, topped with cows, which she'd used for butter and cheese. The sight of them on the dresser shelf took Lou back to her childhood days and the time she had spent in the old kitchen helping make grubby-looking cakes and licking the dishes.

A square tin with a picture of Windsor Castle on its lid held small cherry cakes bursting out of paper cases. Lou set them out on a plate and put the dish on to the prepared tray. It looked elegant; a feast.

She carried the tray back to the living room, gazing round as she set the tray down on a small table beside Janet. It was like being in an antique shop that sold old books too. Some of the items looked valuable and everything gleamed; the air was faintly scented with furniture polish. Janet saw her looking at the bureau.

'It's lovely, so delicate.' Lou said, seeing she had been observed.

'I've always loved it. It was my grandmother's.' Janet laughed suddenly, remembering. 'There's a secret drawer. My mother and I used to leave messages for one another there. Silly ones, really, like "I have a meeting tonight and will be late," or "Going to the shops with Dorothy and we'll have tea together. Don't bother to cook for me."'

Lou was relieved to see her recovering. 'It must have been fun,' she said. 'I'd have loved a secret drawer.'

'It was. Even though the messages were trivial it always felt exciting to open it and see if there was a note for me. Sometimes she put in a bar of chocolate, or I put some sugared almonds for her. She adored those.' She went on, 'Please join me for a cup of tea. You don't have to rush home, do you?'

'I'm fine for a while,' Lou said. 'I work

from home now and I can always catch up in the evening.' She fetched another cup and saucer and a plate.

Janet was still looking at the little bureau. 'There was one just like it on *Antiques Road Show*,' she said. 'Earlier this year. They valued it at an astonishing price. But I could not sell it unless I was desperate and I'm not that yet.'

Lou helped herself to another cake. 'These are delicious,' Lou said. 'My cakes never work. They always sink or taste awful.' She paused, cake halfway to her mouth, realizing that even at this distance she could hear Flyer complaining. 'Can you often hear him shouting like that?' she asked.

'Sometimes I can,' said Janet, frowning. The noise he made irritated her, which was another reason for wishing Lou would get rid of him.

'I'm so sorry,' said Lou. 'He really is the noisiest cat I have ever come across.'

'What on earth made you get him?' Janet asked. She felt ungracious when Lou was being so kind, but she had never imagined having to share her garden with a cat. His arrival still felt like her worst nightmare. And what if he got into the house? She shuddered at the very thought.

'We found him lying in the road,' Lou said. 'We couldn't just leave him. I thought he'd been run over but the vet said he'd been picked up by some kind of hawk and proved too much for him and he was dropped. He was very badly injured.' She paused and looked out of the window, her eyes filling with tears.

Janet, understanding dawning, didn't know what to say.

Lou went on, 'The house has felt so empty since Johnny died and when I found him I just knew that I wanted him to get better and come and live with me.' She thought, with some amazement, that the house was far from empty now. There was a constant presence, who was determined to make her notice him.

'He's only just beginning to be really mobile. That's partly why I walk him on a lead. To strengthen his leg muscles. But he's terrified of outside as well so I'm getting him used to it again. And now I wouldn't be without him. He's such fun – such good company.' She finished her tea and stood up. 'I really must go.'

'I'm sorry,' Janet said. 'I'm being a nuisance.' She didn't just mean about the shopping. She wished she could get on top of her fear and learn to like the little animal as much as Lou obviously did.

Lou lifted the bags, which she had left in the hall by the front door. She carried them into the kitchen. 'These are much too heavy for you,' she said, dismayed. 'Do you always go on the bus to shop?'

'I sold my car,' Janet said, 'so I do have to use the bus now. But I did meet someone – it must have been the day you found the cat. She used to come into the library and she comes over once or twice a month to see her dad. She has taken me sometimes, but I do still need to go out in between. She couldn't come today and I was desperate.'

'You could order on the Internet, and get it delivered,' Lou said.

Janet laughed. 'I hate computers! I had to use one at work and I was so glad to see the back of it! I hate machines. Books give me so much pleasure and I love to collect them. TV or computers just aren't the same. I like the space where you can use your own imagination.'

Lou looked round the room and at the book-filled shelves and shook her head in amazement. 'So many,' she said. 'There are so many I meant to read and never have.'

'I wouldn't worry,' said Janet. 'You can't

read them all! I have special ones that I love to read over and over. Every so often I have a lovely surprise and find a new one.'

'When I try and read now, Flyer insists on sitting on top of the book. The only place I manage it is in bed once he's asleep,' said Lou.

Janet smiled and waved a hand around the room. 'You're welcome to borrow one whenever you want – a library on your doorstep.' She got up and took a slim paperback from a shelf. 'Here, try this. It's the funniest book I have ever read, I think.'

'Thank you!' said Lou, looking down at the cover and reading *Lucky Jim* by Kingsley Amis. 'I'll try it!' she said. 'Now, about your shopping. I can easily take you when I go or I could bring you what you need.'

'I'd love to come with you,' Janet replied. 'It would make it so much easier. As long as I don't have to meet your cat. Listen! He's getting even noisier, if that's possible.'

'I must go back to him. I have the vet's daughter coming while her dad visits the farm, and Susie will wonder what's happened to me. Will you be OK now?'

'I'm much better, thank you. Don't worry. I'll rest a little and then put my shopping away and get a meal. I'll be fine.'

'I'll look in later this evening,' Lou said. She knew she was going to worry lest Janet was so traumatized by Flyer that she suffered from shock.

Jake and Susie arrived as she walked out through Janet's gate, the book in her hand. She hurried up the lane calling, 'Jake! Susie! I'm here!'

'Have you been visiting your neighbour, Lou?' asked Jake.

'Flyer gave her a panic attack,' she said. 'She's terrified of cats. So what do I do now? I don't think he's going to stay close to the house much longer. He's getting adventurous.'

'Maybe Flyer will make her change her mind,' Jake said.

Lou doubted it, and lay awake for some time that night, worrying about Janet. She seemed so lonely and almost housebound. Lou remembered the days before Flyer came. At least she had been able to get out and about, and if she didn't turn up for work her colleagues checked up on her. Who would look out for Janet if something happened? She gave up trying to sleep, put the light on and picked up the book she had been lent. Flyer, tucked up against her, grumbled to himself but soon settled.

When she finally slept she dreamed that Janet was running down the lane with Flyer, three times his normal size, in pursuit. Lou, trying to reach the cat, found her legs refused to move and she could only stand, helpless, as Janet and Flyer vanished into the distance.

She awoke – aware she now had a new worry and no idea how to resolve it. There was no way she could leave Janet to her solitary life. Flyer butted her with his head. He was hungry. His needs came first, he assured her. She would have to watch him and make sure he didn't go visiting down the road when he was more active. She had a sudden vision of him jumping in through Janet's window and giving her the shock of her life.

If only she could find some way of curing her neighbour of her phobia.

But how?

Sixteen

Trish Layton looked at the clock and frowned, saying, 'It looks like Jeff isn't coming today either. When was he last here? It's funny he hasn't been for so long.'

Her husband looked at her. Whatever was preoccupying her, it wasn't amusing. He often wondered how the word 'funny' had come to have a different meaning. Trish found so many things funny. When the hens stopped laying. When the wind blew the old beech tree down. When Silver had a red and white calf, which turned out to be a throwback from long ago.

'It's funny,' Trish said again.

Ben took a drink from the outsize mug he always had when milking was finished and the dairy and yard cleaned. He thought it ugly but his younger son, then only five years old, had given it to him for his birthday. There was a leaping frog in relief on the outside, and when he drained it a much smaller frog stared up at him from the bottom of the mug. Ben said, 'Well, he has been a bit unpredictable since the letter came. I expect he's got a lot to do.'

'Yes, but he's always let me know before.' Trish's hand went to her mouth, her eyes horrified. 'He might have had an accident. That would be awful with his daughter just coming to live with him. When did he say she was coming?'

'He didn't, did he?'

'It's lonely in that cottage. If he were ill, or fell and broke a leg or something, would anyone notice? Maybe we should ring?' she said, obviously worried.

'Trust you always to think the worst,' Ben said, used to his wife's conviction that one cough from a sheep meant foot and mouth, that an off-colour sow was starting swine fever. That bankruptcy was imminent. She'd been the same with the boys. The slightest sign of a temperature and she knew they had meningitis, or some awful disease. Ten minutes late from school and they'd been killed by a car, or abducted by a man intent on murder.

It was an uncomfortable way to live and Ben thought his wife must sometimes exist in a nightmare. Nothing he said seemed to change her. Luckily, it only made the boys laugh. 'There goes Mum, all doom and disaster,' they said and quoted Private Jones at her, from Dad's Army, who always rushed around shouting, 'Don't panic! Don't panic!'

Matt, the eldest, had found an old rhyme and copied it in italics, and given it to her one birthday. He had edged it with little cartoons of disasters. The farm under water. An empty field with cows disappearing over the horizon. Nobody was surprised when he grew up to be a cartoonist. Ben collected the daily papers in which they appeared and had a large scrapbook of which he was extremely proud. The rhyme, now somewhat tired with time, still hung on the wall: 'When in danger, when in doubt, run in circles, scream and shout.' Trish had thought it funny and, that time, she really had meant amusing.

'You never ought to have been a farmer's wife.' Ben often said. 'Scare a minute, with you.' It was true that there was so much scope for crisis on a farm. He wondered if other occupations would have provided the same opportunity for worry. Certainly there would have been with the children, whatever their father's profession. Ben was sure it stemmed from his wife's childhood and a mother who overprotected her from all kinds of real and imaginary dangers. His mother-in-law never visited the farm because she was sure she would fall victim to some dreadful disease or accident. She just knew the bull would escape and kill everybody.

All the same, there was no one like Trish in a crisis. She coped immediately, dealing with injured children and animals with great efficiency, even if she did fear the worst that could happen.

Trish got up from the table suddenly. Tass, the big, ginger tomcat, was trying to open the window wider so that he could get in to steal one of the scones put on a plate on the sill to cool. He tried daily. Lack of success never defeated hope.

Trish banged on the window; he hissed at her and fled. Neither liked the other. Good ratter, but nobody's friend, was what Trish often said. She turned to look towards the gate as Brig the collie began to bark.

'Well, well, here's the man himself. He's come by car. That's a first,' Trish said, calling to Brig, who stopped barking and lay on the step, his eyes baleful. He was used to Jeff on foot. The car was unfamiliar and Jeff wasn't alone.

'He has a passenger with him. It must be his daughter.' Ben watched the child, still sitting in the car. About ten years old? She was a pretty child, slim and dark with a grey, crocheted hat pulled down on her head. When she turned her head to look at Jeff, Ben saw that there was a bright-blue flower on the side.

Sandy was reluctant to leave the car. She was a city child. She missed the New York buildings that towered into the air and shone like fairyland in the early dawn. They had only been in England for six weeks. Everything was strange. She had to get used to a new accent, and to different words for things she had known so well. Like bonnet for a car instead of hood. And trunk instead of boot, and she'd never get used to calling cookies biscuits. Why call a fender a bumper?

London had been daunting enough but the countryside had its own intimidations. There was so much of it, fields and woods stretching forever, with no friendly streets and no lights and so few people.

Now there were all those cows and they looked so big. She had never seen live farm animals before. There had been the donkey but that was long ago and he had always been safely in the field. The fences looked strong enough, but suppose the cows charged? The dog looked fierce, and his barking frightened her. Suppose he attacked her?

She had hated the flight to England. It had been bumpy and when the plane plunged she had been sure it was going to crash. Her mother had felt ill and slept most of the way and she didn't want to wake her. In the past year she had learned to endure so much on her own.

She hadn't liked London. It was noisy and smelly and wherever they'd gone there'd been long hours spent in taxis, crawling through the streets. The people she'd met there had seemed unable to decide quite how to treat her. Some had behaved as if she were adult, while others had made her feel like a small girl who could not share in adult preoccupations.

The hotel where they had stayed was horrible: their room small and basic, the beds uncomfortable and the food unappetizing. Money, Sandy knew, was another problem, and she'd worried lest they run right out. Where would they go then? Prison? Was it a crime to have no money? Suppose her father didn't want her? What would happen to her then?

The staff had treated Sandy as if she did not exist – except for the hotel owner who had told her she must behave herself or they'd have to leave. She had wondered how she *could* misbehave. The last year, and having to do so much for her mother, had turned her into a sober child. There had been nobody who cared. Life had been far from easy after her stepfather died.

'Your grandfather threw all his money away so there was nothing left when he went,' Kate had said one day, when Sandy was about seven. Sandy had wondered why on earth he would have done anything so silly. And where had he thrown it? She could not remember her grandparents. Her grandmother had died a few weeks before they went to America, her grandfather when she was six. Her mother had hoped there would be money left for them, but there was none. She had had to save hard for the fares to England and for their stay when they arrived. It had been worse when she could no longer work. Mike had been insured, but it was far from enough for their needs.

'Where did grandfather throw his money?' she had asked her stepfather, a few weeks before he too died.

He had laughed at her. 'He threw it down gold mines, but they were never real. Just fairy gold,' Mike had said.

That puzzled her even more. Mike liked to tease and she was never sure he meant what he said.

It felt like she'd spent her first weeks in England sitting outside closed doors while her mother talked secrets. She'd learned to take a book with her so that she could lose herself, not think about what was happening. It had been her only relief.

There had been so many people to see. Doctors. Specialists. Hospitals. Social workers, whatever they were. Her mother had done her best to tell her what was going on, but it had all been bewildering.

Until her mother had been sure about her father, the social workers had talked about care, or foster parents. Sometimes Sandy thought the visitors forgot she was there. She had often sat silent – anxious not to be excluded from the discussions but not understanding them either. She'd felt as if she had wandered into a strange world where nothing made sense, only too aware that her mother was becoming worse. She'd felt like a parcel, tossed around without any control over where she might end up.

Beth, from the hospice, had been a lifeline. She had made those last two weeks almost fun. 'I'll be looking after your mother,' she had said. 'I'll be here every day so you can get to know me, and not worry about her. She'll be among friends. Meanwhile, she wants to show you all sorts of things while she can. I'll come with you both when you go to your father.'

They had gone to London Zoo where Beth had pushed her mother in a wheelchair. They visited the British Museum and also the Planetarium. She'd been fascinated by that. All those stars and all that space. It had made her feel so small – a tiny speck in a vast universe. Beth had bought her a book on astronomy. There were no stars in the London sky but she'd thought that maybe in the country they would be visible.

Sandy was glad that she knew Beth before she and her mother had to part for good. It felt like a connection even when they could no longer be together. She knew that was coming. Or thought she did. It was hard to realize. She hadn't wanted to think of it.

Her mother would be so lonely without her. She hoped Beth would make her goodnight drink and bring her tea in the morning.

That first night Jeff had finally fallen asleep in his chair, exhausted, just after five o'clock. He woke at nine, to find Sandy shaking him gently by the shoulder.

It was the way she had always wakened her mother. 'Time to get up, Dad. I'm cooking your breakfast.'

He was only half-awake and for a moment was unable to collect his thoughts. He had a headache, and did not really want to eat but he couldn't disappoint her. He wondered whether to hug her, but she distanced herself, behaving like a polite visitor. 'You didn't need to make my breakfast, love,' he said, aching for her.

'I wanted to. I've had to do it all the time till we came to the hotel. Mum's been unable to do it for nearly a year ... ever since I was nine. We didn't know at first what was wrong. Her hands were so shaky and she dropped things or burnt herself. She told me what to do. I love cooking. I'm good at it.'

It wasn't a brag but a matter of fact.

She had woken in the night, worrying about her tears. Her father might not want her if she cried. Cooking breakfast like she had done for Mum would make her useful to him.

Jeff decided that they would drive to the farm after breakfast. He couldn't expect the child to walk two miles to the farm and back again. He showered and shaved and dressed and came down to find the table laid: a place mat he had not seen before surrounded by cutlery, with a plate beside it. There was marmalade in a dish that she must have unearthed from the back of the dresser, and butter on a saucer.

He was amazed to be presented with bacon, eggs, tomatoes, fried bread and two slices of toast. That was the sort of thing he sometimes cooked for lunch. His usual breakfast was either toast or cereal.

The phone call came as he mopped the last of the yolk up with his toast. 'Hello, Beth?' he said.

Sandy stopped in her tracks, watching her father's face. When he looked over at her, his eyes filled with tears. She watched one slide from under his glasses and down one cheek. She ran upstairs.

Jeff put the phone down and slowly followed her.

Beth had said, 'She just slipped away in the night. It was as though she knew Sandy was safe and she could let go.'

'Why does God let it happen?' Sandy asked that night at bedtime. 'I thought He was kind and would answer our prayers. He hasn't answered mine. And if He's kind, why does He allow such awful wars and so many people suffering?'

He hasn't answered my prayers either, Jeff thought. Except one: that I should get my daughter back. Who was it said be careful what you pray for as you may get it, but not the way you wanted?

'Maybe he really is like a father,' Jeff said. 'I can't make it easier for you ... just be there for you. Nobody can alter life for other people by taking on their pain.'

He sat long into the night, listening for sobs. He crept into her room several times but she seemed to be sound asleep. It added to his own pain, looking down at the child's quiet face and thinking of her wakening to the knowledge that her mother had gone forever. Perhaps the reality had not yet dawned? Perhaps constant worry was numbing and she had already done her grieving?

He felt grief himself and guilt that Kate had suffered for so long without contacting him. He could have been there for them, could have helped financially. But she had always been proud and insisted on doing things her way.

Could he have made a difference?

He didn't know.

So he hadn't been to the farm that day, nor for the next week. Now Kate's funeral was over and it was time for them to find a way to move on.

'Come on, Sandy,' Jeff said. 'There might be tea and hot scones and jam and cream. They often have that after milking.' He was painfully aware that she must be finding this difficult. He felt he had to watch every word, had to find inducements for her, and he did not know how. It was a new form of agony to have to watch her pain.

He realized, as he climbed out into the yard and saw his daughter's anxious face, that she was afraid of the farm animals. He took her hand and led her into the kitchen. A tabby cat, sitting in a patch of sunlight washing herself, saw them and fled.

Sandy loved the kitchen as soon as she saw it. She had never seen anything like it. It was the heart of the house. Big armchairs placed round the Aga, a huge scrubbed table against one wall, and a battered dresser filled with plates, each bearing the picture of a horse. There were model horses on shelves around the room, to which were pinned dozens of rosettes. The shelves held silver salvers, cups and shields.

She was aware of three big men, all looking at her. Brad, the tanker driver, was about to leave. He nodded as he went out. Brig put his nose into the opening door, but was pushed away to resume his post. Ben and Joe, the cowman, smiled at her. She tried to smile back but it was hard.

Sandy liked the woman who, dressed in fawn trousers and a fawn jersey, reminded her of a big, cuddly teddy bear.

'This is Sandy, my daughter. She's been with me for ten days now,' Jeff said. He took her hand and said, 'We haven't been for a while because Kate died the day after she left Sandy with me.'

A sob escaped from Sandy and she quickly bit it back. Jeff put his arm round her and held her close, and then passed her his hanky.

Trish said, 'Oh Jeff, I am sorry. We wondered where you were.' She came and put her arms round them both in an enveloping hug.

Joe, always sensitive to people's and animals' feelings, stood up. 'We've got little pigs outside,' he said. 'They're only a few hours old. Would you like to see them?'

'She needs wellies. The yard's filthy,' Trish said. She went into the scullery and produced the smallest she could find, adding thick socks to pad them out. They watched Sandy, dwarfed by Joe, as the two walked across the yard.

Joe had three children of his own. Paul was about the same age as this child. He sensed her desperate unhappiness.

Luckily, Minnie the big sow was amiable and didn't mind her new litter being inspected. 'What a lot of piglets,' Sandy said, watching the wriggling line of little bodies busily sucking at the enormous sow's teats. 'However many are there?'

'Fifteen,' Joe said. 'Eight boys and seven girls.'

'Gosh! I didn't know they had so many.'

'They don't usually. This is almost one for the record books. Most of ours have around ten at the most.'

'I wish I had a brother or sister,' Sandy said, with such longing in her voice.

'You must find it –' Joe paused. He had been about to say frightening, but it was not an idea to put into her head. Instead, he substituted – 'very different. Did you enjoy living in America?'

'I did till Mike died. Only, then it got

difficult as Mum had to go to work and there was never quite enough money, so we had to move into a tiny apartment. Then Mum got ill. She was saving for our fares back to England. It took such a long time and she kept getting worse.'

Joe wondered how many ten-year-olds were burdened with such worries. 'Let's go back for your scones,' he said. 'Have you ever had hot scones with jam and cream?'

Sandy had never had scones of any sort and she wondered what they were.

Back in the kitchen, Trish sat down beside Jeff. 'You must have had a really tough week,' she said sympathetically.

Jeff nodded. 'Sandy took it really hard. She knew it was coming but not so suddenly. It was too much, coming to me and then Kate dying, all in less than a day.'

'Poor little moppet.' Trish said, feeling an overwhelming sadness. Life was not going to be easy for either Jeff or Sandy.

Jeff went on, 'She did come to terms with it a bit when she understood that Kate had been hanging on to see her settled. She was glad that Kate had met me again and seen where she would be living. And she was glad that Kate wouldn't be hurting any more.'

Trish hesitated, but felt that she might be

able to offer some comfort. She foresaw large problems for Jeff, but did not think Ben would mind if she provided some assistance. 'Look … if you need any help … I've always wanted a daughter and I'd be happy to mother her a bit, do the girly things with her.' She chuckled. 'To be honest, it would make a change to have some female company instead of all these males I'm surrounded by.'

Jeff laughed. 'Thanks for the offer, Trish. I'm just muddling through, like you said I would. So I'm not sure what she needs at the moment. Can we take it a day at a time? There's so much for her to get used to.'

'Of course,' said Trish. 'Just keep bringing her across with you so that we can get to know each other and I guess the rest will follow if it's meant to. If she seems comfortable here you can always leave her with me so you can get some time to yourself.'

'It seems an imposition,' he said, hating to find himself indebted.

'Don't be daft,' said Trish. 'You don't have to do it alone. That's what friends are for, you silly man.' She laughed to take the sting out of her words and Jeff grinned at her, feeling better than he had for several weeks.

Joe came in with Sandy, her eyes bright

with excitement. 'They're sweet,' she said. 'So little, and so busy. They can run around and their eyes are open, and they're not a day old yet. There are fifteen of them. Joe let me hold one. He wriggled and squealed.'

Trish handed her a plate and said, 'Help yourself to a scone.'

Sandy looked at the jam dish and the bowl of cream and asked, 'What do I do with those?'

Jeff showed her and Sandy watched in amazement as he spread a large spoonful of jam across the split scone and topped it with a dollop of thick cream. He handed it to her and said, 'Go on, try that!'

Sandy bit into it. Cream dripped down her chin and she wiped it off with a finger and licked it. 'Mmm, delicious,' she said, and promptly demolished it. 'Please, can I have another?'

'Nothing wrong with your appetite.' Trish laughed as she filled a tin with cakes and added, 'You can take these home with you.'

'I need to sort out a school,' Jeff said. 'I should have done it before, but there's been so much to do.'

'My son's the same age as Sandy,' Joe said. 'He's in the top class of the primary school next year ... I would think that's where she'll go. I can help you sort that out.'

Sandy did not want to think about school. She had another priority – something she felt sure would help her in the weeks to come. 'You said we could look for a donkey.'

Jeff had forgotten. 'I wondered if we could find one and put it in the field at the end of my garden,' he said.

'There's an easier solution. I've three here,' Ben said, 'and one of them is about to foal.' He looked at Sandy, her face alight with excitement. 'Why don't you both come and see them now. You could have the baby for your own if you like and come and look after him here. Then when you are at school he'll still have company. Donkeys like to have their mates around.'

Jeff and Trish smiled across the table at each other.

Jeff's normal routine seemed to have been interrupted for good. He would have to work out a new way to ensure he found time to work. No point in hurrying home now. He'd not be able to write a word. The next Donko book awaited him but the title page was still a blank. He followed the others, through the yard where horses peered over their stable doors, cows gathered near the barn and hens pecked everywhere. Joe led them behind the barn and into another field. At the far end was a wooden shed and beside it grazed three donkeys. He called to them and they trotted across, eager to see if food was on offer. One of them was huge with the foal she was carrying.

Sandy gazed in adoration. She couldn't believe it. A baby donkey for her very own. 'What are they called?' she asked.

'Ruby, Pearl and Jasper. Ruby's the one who's about to be a mum and Jasper is Pearl's son.'

'When is the baby due?' Sandy asked eagerly.

'Towards the end of next week, we think,' Ben replied.

Sandy clapped her hands in delight and leant against Jeff. 'Something to look forward to, Dad,' she said.

Seventeen

Sandy sat contentedly in the car on the way home; in spite of her fears she had loved the farm. The thought of going to see the donkeys, having one of her own, filled her with happiness. Everyone had been so kind, unlike the visitors her mother had had at the hotel. Though they hadn't exactly been unkind. They had just ignored her. She liked the cottage, and knew her father cared deeply about her, but frequent thoughts of her mother saddened her.

Jeff was worried. Sandy seemed to have settled into his life as if she had lived there forever, but she was subdued and often silent, staring into the distance. He had never imagined such a tidy or self-contained child. Her bedroom was always immaculate, the bed made, and the clothes put neatly away in the drawers. She made his bed as well, and tidied away the laundry into the Ali Baba basket on the landing.

'Please show me how to use the washing

machine,' she'd said. 'It's not like ours.'

'You don't have to do the washing, love,' Jeff had replied.

'I need things to do. To stop me thinking.'

He wondered what she was thinking and wished she would talk, but apart from necessary conversation she said little. As the days went by, she liked him to read to her each night, always wanting one of the Donko stories. They were far too young for her, but they seemed to amuse and comfort her. A link with her mother, perhaps?

She seemed to be trying her best not be obtrusive.

He was unaware of her night-time worries after he had kissed her and gone downstairs. She always went to bed at nine. Jeff tried to write then, wanting to keep the days for her, and to fill them to keep her mind from her mother's death.

They spent time at the farm. They went for walks. They sat by the river, watching for a kingfisher, and were rewarded by a brief flash of brilliant blue. Trish took Sandy shopping for winter clothes. She needed almost a complete wardrobe, as she seemed to be growing fast.

But Sandy still had a major worry – one she was afraid to share. Nobody knew she had overheard the senior social worker on their last day in London. Sandy had been sent downstairs to read but had come back, not liking to be alone amongst strangers. The hotel clientele were mostly elderly and did not appreciate the presence of a child. The little passage at the entrance to the room housed the bathroom, and Sandy slipped inside. The door to the bedroom was ajar.

Eileen Frith was a prim woman, soon to retire. She had been brought up by a timid mother and a father who was sure that a just God visited his wrath on the unworthy. Divorce was a crime, as was remarriage.

Eileen had little time for Kate, who had committed two of the worst sins and was now being punished for it. It had been most remiss of her to have a child and to fail to provide that child with relatives. Furthermore, she should not give in to her feelings. Eileen had no idea how much pain Kate was suffering. The social worker was limited by a complete lack of empathy for other people, and by her own strict code of life.

There were days when Kate, in agony, could do little but take the painkillers and lie on her bed. This Eileen regarded as pure self-indulgence. The woman should at least try for the child's sake. Nor should she have come back to England to take advantage of the National Health Service. Too many from abroad did that. She did not like children, in spite of her job, and she terrified Sandy.

'You would do much better to arrange for the child to go into care,' Sandy heard her say, the woman's precise, uninflected voice carrying loudly through the open bedroom door to where Sandy was sitting. 'How do you know your ex-husband will want her, or even be kind to her? You haven't been in touch with this man for six years. He may not even be alive.'

'He is. I got his address from his agent.'

'I understand he is a writer. Such an unpredictable way to earn a living. Does he have a real job? He may not want the child. Or find, after a few months, that he can't manage her. Then she would have to go into care. It would be better to do so at once.'

The social worker had gone at last. Sandy hated her, and everything about her. Her prim clothes, always brown, relieved by a white blouse, worn with a tie. Her hair was plaited and worn on top of her head, and she had rimless glasses and eyes that seemed to bore into your soul. A voice that seemed always to condemn.

Sandy had not told her mother she had overheard the conversation but now, lying in bed, she wondered if her father really would tire of her and she would have to go into care. What was care? She imagined herself in some terrible orphanage, like those Dickens wrote about. If she did everything to help him, if she was quiet and obedient and did her best, perhaps he wouldn't tire of her. Only maybe it wasn't what he wanted from her.

She wanted her mother. If she hadn't gone to live with her father, perhaps she would still be alive.

'If only we could do something,' Jeff said to Trish on one of their farm visits. His daughter seemed more relaxed there, loving the donkeys and behaving more like a child than an adult. Trish had insisted they stayed for lunch, and Sandy had been well occupied, helping. Joe had taken her to feed carrots to the donkeys. Her own foal had been born several weeks ago now. She had been there to see her first wobbly steps, her first feed. The little animal was knobbly kneed and charming, her coat dark grey and thick, her muzzle white. Huge, brown eyes gazed at them and Sandy had fallen instantly in love. She'd decided to call her

Amelia and couldn't wait to see her every day.

Sandy didn't worry so much when she was at the farm and found that she could have long, whispered conversations with her own donkey when nobody was around to listen. The little animal would gaze up at her, her ears pricked, and then suddenly take off round the field, prancing and jumping with the sheer joy of life. How Sandy wished she felt like that.

Eighteen

Flyer woke and stretched slowly. The fur on his shoulders was slowly growing back – a large patch of pale, short fur in which the scars from the attack still showed faintly. With the soreness long gone and his bones healed, the immediate memory of the attack had faded.

The inside of Lou's house now held no mysteries for him. He had his favourite places: warm patches on the floor where central heating pipes ran underneath; dark corners in which to lurk and pounce; secret spaces under furniture where he could pretend a mouse was hiding. The window sill in the living room where he could sit and look out at the world, pretending he was still a brave, intrepid hunter in fear of nothing.

Outside it was a different matter. The open spaces of the garden terrified him and he dared only to prowl around the edges, ears pricked for every sound and eyes alert, watching for danger. The rustle of a branch, a leaf blowing on the wind, the fluttering wings of a bird, would all send him diving deep into cover where he would crouch, ears back, his tail bushed and trembling.

He stayed there for hours sometimes, terrifying Lou with the thought that he had been abducted again. Eventually, she found his habitual hiding places and enticed him out with tasty morsels of food. His confidence did slowly increase, not because he lost his fear but because he became familiar with the routes that were safe, providing enough cover for him to feel safe from danger.

His behaviour saddened Lou. But then, too, she was glad of his caution. It kept him away from the birds and she felt she really didn't have to worry because he so clearly knew how to keep himself safe.

Gradually, he widened his horizons. He felt the lure of the bigger world, could smell the enticements on the wind, but nothing from the world of the wild was strong enough to overcome his fear. People, however, were different. He trusted them and, just as in his previous life at Stone's Throw Farm, he wanted to get to know them. Lou and Jake, and Ray and Susie were all his willing slaves, his listeners, his play mates and his comfort. But at the edges of his world he knew there were others.

The sight of Janet in her garden one day was too much to resist. He wanted to get to know her. Stepping out from the security of the hedgerow he sat in a patch of sunshine and began to wash himself. She didn't notice him so he yowled loudly, just to say hello. She dropped her trowel and jumped to her feet, shouting at the top of her voice, 'Go away you horrible animal. Go away!' She didn't come close to him but waved her arms wildly in the air.

He crouched and ran for cover. He was not put off. After all, he had grown used to Mark in his previous life, so he knew she wasn't a danger to be kept away from. It was more a matter of tactics. His curiosity about her must be satisfied; he must make friends with her and he would find a way to do it.

The branch of an apple tree in Janet's garden was close against her kitchen window. Flyer had enough strength now to clamber up the trunk and onto the low branch, and it wasn't too far to jump down.

There, crouching on the branch a few days later, he watched while she prepared her breakfast, ate it at the little counter and then washed up and tidied the room. His eyes followed her as she ate, from plate to spoon to mouth and back again.

She looked up one day and saw those blue eyes staring at her. She stopped in horror, hand halfway to mouth. The spoon shook and the cereal tumbled back into the bowl. She leapt up and banged on the window, shouting, 'Go away!'

He jumped down and ran off, and she sighed with relief. When Lou took her shopping the next day she didn't dare confess she had frightened Flyer away. What would Lou think of her?

After that, Flyer often crouched under the hedge between her and Lou's garden. He made no move towards her, yet he was obviously fascinated by her. As long as they regarded each other from a safe distance she could just about tolerate him.

He was a handsome, almost fully-grown, cat now, with only a trace of a limp. His points had darkened to a chocolate brown and he was long-legged and elegant. His strength returned, he ran and climbed, jumped and played with anything he could find. One day it was a frog sitting in the middle of the lawn. He didn't think it was good to eat but the way it jumped when he tapped it on the back with a paw was irresistible. He stalked it across the lawn until Lou, seeing him in pursuit, rushed to rescue the frog and take it back to the stream.

Lou told Ray about it and he laughed. 'Maybe he hoped it would turn into a pretty female cat when he kissed it,' he said.

He had been full of laughter the last few weeks and Lou suspected that romance was in the air. She wondered if he had met someone at the 'Young Farmers' Christmas party. If he had, he had kept quiet about it. But those, Lou knew, were often the important ones.

Flyer's instinctive feel for distress had been heightened by his own experiences and he had an agenda of his own when it came to comforting unhappy people. He knew when Lou was having bad days – days when something reminded her of Johnny, or a programme mentioned 9/11. She never heard that phrase without a flashback to that dreadful event. Even though so much had changed since Flyer came to live with her, there were still times when her loss felt unbearable. Those days, he didn't go out. Curled up on Lou's lap he licked her hand and purred, putting up a paw to pat her face. She found it as good as a hug and relaxed into the comfort of his solid warmth.

He seemed to know, too, if Ray or Jake had had a bad day and then he would desert her to snuggle up against whichever man happened to be there. She began to sense their moods herself, triggered by his reaction. Susie, too, was a target for his attention. She divided her time between Lou and farm visits with Jake when she wasn't at school. She cuddled him as if he were a teddy bear, burying her face in his soft fur, obviously soothed by his presence and his ready purr.

Flyer did have a deep need to make sure the people around him were happy. Misery overwhelmed him, and he felt he had to do something, anything, to make it go away. Sometimes he would do it by trying to play one of his games, bringing a paper ball, rubbing against legs, rolling, making his presence felt. He knew how to make people laugh, how to energize them with his antics, as well as how to make them relax.

Nowadays Jake often called in briefly if he went to any of the three local farms, but she was surprised to see him, one Monday, arriving as she was making her mid morning cup of coffee. Flyer jumped up as soon as Jake came in.

'Coffee?' Lou asked.

Jake lowered himself carefully into one of the armchairs, as if he was hurting. 'Please. And –' he looked at her, sorrow in his eyes – 'silence for a few minutes.'

'Bad day?' Lou asked.

'Appalling.'

Lou, always quick to think of trouble, visualized a variety of disasters. She longed to ask what had happened, but Jake looked exhausted. *He's always tired*, she thought. He sipped at his coffee, and as soon as he put the mug down on the table, Flyer jumped to him and cuddled against him, his head on Jake's shoulder.

'No surgery?' she asked, glancing at the clock.

'It was a light one, luckily, and the two operations can wait till this afternoon. Two cats to spay.' He sighed, running his fingers back through his hair, and said, 'I had to escape.'

Lou buttered a scone and spread it with raspberry jam. Food for comfort. Was Susie ill? Or had she had an accident on her bike?

Flyer nestled up against Jake's warm Aran jersey, and then, very gently, reached out a paw and tapped Jake's cheek. Jake was more than usually unhappy and Lou resisted the desire to go to him and hold him, comforting him with her arms around him. In the last few weeks, it wasn't the first time she had felt the need. She almost envied the cat. It was so much more straightforward for him. No risks involved ... or none he worried his little, furry head about.

The cuckoo clock door opened and the bird popped out. Flyer sat up to listen. He could never understand the bird that came out so unpredictably and then disappeared again.

'He's never got used to it,' Lou said, and Jake smiled at the cat. Both ears were pricked forward, his head on one side. Every time the bird called they twitched. When it called for the tenth time, Flyer climbed on to Jake's shoulder and stretched himself up the wall, trying to get at the bird.

'He definitely has designs on it,' Jake said. 'Don't leave a chair near it!' He drank his coffee and relaxed. There was always peace in Lou's home, and he sought it more and more often. Life at the surgery was frantic. Susie was less than easy. Awkward age, his mother said when he spoke on the phone. She lived too far away to help. All ages seemed awkward, Jake thought.

Alison seemed to be becoming more and more clingy, following him around, asking eternal questions and offering to take Susie out to the shops or to the cinema. Susie refused to go with her. She would rather be at the farms or with Lou. No way would she go out with Alison. If he insisted it ended with a shouting match and slammed doors.

Here at Lou's he could unwind, sit back in the big arm chair, and be soothed by both Flyer and Lou. She was undemanding, and could sit in silence without fretting, not wanting his every action explained. He enjoyed Lou's company more than he would have thought possible a few months ago, and looked forward to the time he spent with her. If only he didn't always have to be working. He wanted to ask her if she would like to go for a meal with him ... but what if she said no? All this would be spoilt. It wouldn't just be for him, but Susie too. She enjoyed Lou's company and was a different girl when she came here.

He had to admit that Alison was interested in the treatment of the animals, but at times her constant barrage of questions exhausted him – especially after a difficult operation, when all he wanted was to be quiet and listen to music. He could lose himself – letting the sounds wash over him, obliterating the world.

Alison, who was tone deaf, infuriated him by talking when he had put on a favourite piece. She felt silence was a crime, that he was in need of cheering up, and she was so obviously sure that her chatter amused him. One day, he thought, he'd lose his temper and yell at her, but he knew she meant well. One of the worst things anyone could say about anyone else, he thought.

He lay back, savouring the room. The colours soothed. A vase of anemones brightened a dull corner. Above the mantel hung a seascape; five dolphins leaped from the water, their arched bodies curving against the sky. It would be good to be on a boat, far away from here, watching the dolphins and whales as they frolicked in the sunshine.

He did not want to think.

He knew Lou was wondering why he had called at such an unusual time.

'I had clients with a very large dog,' he said at last. 'I've been warning them for months that it was too strong for the children to take out but they wouldn't listen. "He goes to dog class and he's good," was all they would ever say. Today their eleven-year-old took him out before school. The dog saw a cat across the road and dived for it. The boy had the lead wrapped round his wrist and had no choice but to follow. The dog got across. The child is dead. He went under a lorry. I've just put the dog to sleep. Why don't people listen?'

'That's terrible,' Lou said, thinking of the bereaved family. They would always blame themselves.

As if to comfort him, Flyer stood up, turned round several times and then cuddled up again.

'It was an accident waiting to happen,' Jake said. 'Only why in heaven's name did the child have to die and not the dog? The dog was a very healthy two-year-old, and Alison hasn't stopped crying since I put him down. The family didn't ever want to see him again and can you blame them? There was no way I could rehome him. He had never had the training that would make him manageable. Why don't people realize that even the smallest dog needs to be taught manners, and be civilized?'

Jake had known the boy well. Paul always came with his father or mother when the dog came in for treatment. A bright child, with a wonderful beaming smile and ready laughter.

'I think I'll be a vet like you,' he had said last time they came. Now he had gone forever, leaving distraught parents. It had taken all Jake's self-control not to shout at them, to rail at them with fury, saying, 'I told you so. Why didn't you listen to me?'

It was no use.

He'd liked the dog. Sultan only needed a firm hand and training. He'd lain on the table, trusting, when the needle plunged in. Alison had not stopped sobbing. Jake had had to escape.

He sighed as the clock struck the half hour. 'Flyer is the most soothing animal I have ever met,' he said. 'I think I need to borrow him.'

'You can have him for a day,' she said generously. 'I'd never have believed a cat could become so much a part of one's life. He's made so much of a difference.'

Jake looked at her. 'I think I'd rather visit here for a day, and enjoy you *and* the cat.'

Lou looked startled, his words an echo of her thoughts. She blushed and, seeking to hide her confusion, said, 'He has a downside though; he's such a mischievous monkey at times. My bottom stair carpet looks as if it's been clawed to pieces and he keeps climbing on the mantelpiece to knock the ornaments off.'

'He's still young. He'll grow up and then you'll want his kitten days back again.' Jake stroked the soft fur. 'He's made a miraculous recovery. At least we did well with this one.'

Lou guessed his thoughts. She put a hand on his arm. 'Jake, you did your best. You told them. I think you'd feel much worse if you hadn't warned them. We're not responsible for other people's actions.' *If only*, she thought, visions of planes flying into the towers flashing across her mind.

Flyer yowled, wanting to change their mood.

'He's agreeing with me,' Lou said.

Jake stood up, and put the cat down gently in the place he had just vacated. Flyer stretched and then turned round a couple of times before settling down again into the warm spot Jake had left.

'Jobs to do. I could stay here forever. You're my haven,' Jake said. He hesitated, wanting to tell her more clearly how much she was beginning to mean to him. Then he saw Johnny looking at him from his photograph. Maybe it was too soon. She had shown no sign that he meant more to her than a friend, nor responded to his remark about spending the day with her.

Lou, aware of what was in his mind, felt unsure of herself, of what she wanted. Too unsure to say anything, yet knowing that she would miss him so much if he and Susie stopped coming.

'Do you mind me calling?' he asked suddenly.

'I love you calling,' Lou said, realizing how true that was. She watched from the window as he drove away, wishing she could wave a wand and ease his life. If only he could find a partner at his veterinary practice. It was too much for one man.

Jake bought himself a sandwich at the supermarket and pulled into a lay-by to eat it in the car, not wanting to face Alison. At least the other girl left him in peace.

'I told you before. She wants to marry you, Dad,' Susie had said, only the evening before, when he'd finally shut the door on the woman, and sighed with relief.

'I still think that's ridiculous,' Jake said.

But was it? If it was so then it was a pipe dream. A life with Alison would be impossible. Everything she did grated on him and he often wished he had a reason to replace her. But she did her work extremely well.

Lou washed the mugs, and made herself a snack lunch. Flyer was restless and when she opened the back door he went out into the garden, diving at once for the cover of a bush. He peered out at her and yowled. He sat there for some time, his eyes focused, and Lou wondered if maybe a mouse had its hole there. Once he put out a tentative paw, as if trying to feel down the hole. Thwarted, he came in.

'You're just one big interruption,' Lou told him as he jumped to the arm of the chair beside her desk, and then to the desk and tried to catch her pen as she wrote down the figures for the farm accounts that had just been given her.

Flyer yowled.

'Obviously, you agree,' she said and laughed as he decided that he wanted her lap. 'You're a pest,' she said, 'but I wouldn't be without you.' The difference he had made was unbelievable and she had only had him for five months.

She was glad of his company that night. She could not get Jake out of her mind. He was so passionate about the animals he tended, and he had obviously been fond of the child who had died. He had had a younger brother. How must the family feel, she wondered.

It was a long time before she slept, lulled at last by Flyer's soothing purr.

Nineteen

Sandy opened the study door and asked, 'How's it going, Dad? Have you got any ideas yet?'

Jeff grimaced and tapped his head with his knuckles. 'Nope. My head is empty. Come on, let's go outside. Would you like to play French cricket while the sun's shining?'

'Ooh, yes,' said Sandy and dashed off to get the bat and ball.

Jeff sat for a moment staring at the blank

page on the screen. His publisher had been on the phone again wanting to know when he could expect the book. 'We agreed November,' he'd said indignantly, 'and it's February now.'

Jeff had fobbed him off with half-truths. 'Yes it's going well. Yes, in a couple of months. No, there's no problem.'

Oh well, maybe he'd think better after a bit of exercise. He pulled on his shoes at the back door and Sandy threw the tennis ball to him.

'Me, first, Dad. Me first.'

He smiled and wished she would relax like that more often. She took up her stance in the middle of the back garden. He tossed the ball and she missed. It landed behind her in the flower bed and he jogged over to fetch it. 'Remember you can't turn round, Sandy,' he said.

'I know,' she replied, twisting sideways.

Jeff feinted left and right with the ball, Sandy swiping wildly. The ball hit her leg and Jeff shouted 'OUT!'

'Go on, Dad. Let me have another go,' she begged.

'OK,' said Jeff. 'We'll pretend that was a practice.'

Sandy grinned and turned to face Jeff

again. He threw the ball and it landed sweetly in the centre of her bat. She timed it perfectly, hitting the ball so that it sailed high into the air, over the hedge, way over next-door's garden to land somewhere near the house.

'Wow,' said Jeff. 'They'll be wanting you on the village cricket team if they see you hitting like that.'

Sandy laughed. 'It was a good one, wasn't it? Come on, Dad. Let's go and see how far it went.' She ran up the garden and out into the lane, looking for the fluorescent yellow of the ball.

There was no sign of it and after a few minutes Jeff said, 'Never mind, Sandy. There's another one in the porch.'

She shouted and pointed, 'Look, there it is. It's rolled under the gate of The Bramble Patch and down to the front door. Can I go and get it?'

'Go on then. But be quick.'

Sandy unlatched the gate and walked down the path. She stopped suddenly, staring in disbelief. Crouched at the edge of the path was a cat. He turned his head and she saw blue eyes in a dark face. He turned back to stare at the ball, wiggled his rear end and pounced. Sandy exclaimed in delight. 'Dad,

Dad. Look at this cat. He's got blue eyes.'

The front door of the cottage opened and Janet appeared. She took one look at the scene and shouted, 'Go away, go away. I don't want you here.'

Sandy backed off, her lower lip trembling and tears in her eyes. The cat ran off up the lane. Jeff swung open the gate and strode down the path. He put one arm round Sandy and said, 'I'm sorry, we didn't mean to upset you. I'm Jeff from The Twisted Willows and this is my daughter Sandy. We just came to get the ball.' He picked it up and turned to go.

Janet looked stricken. 'I'm so sorry. It wasn't you I was upset about. It was the cat. I don't want him near me or in my garden. I know he's handsome but I just hate cats.' She looked embarrassed and said to Sandy, 'Actually, it's worse than that. I'm frightened of them.'

Sandy said nothing. She understood being frightened of cows or bulls, but a cat? A small, furry cat? She ran a finger over her eyes to wipe away the tears that had threatened.

Janet said again, 'I'm so sorry, Sandy. I didn't mean to upset you. Why don't you both come in and have a drink and a bite to eat with me?' She held out her hand and introduced herself. 'I'm Janet Leigh, by the way. Call me Janet.'

Jeff shook her hand and said, 'Thank you. It's about time we got to know each other. What do you think, Sandy?'

She nodded in agreement and Janet took them through the house. 'We could sit outside since it's such a lovely day,' Janet said. 'I know it's only February but it's quite warm in the sun. It seems a shame to be inside. What would you like to drink? I have home-made lemonade and ginger beer, or there's tea or coffee?'

'Ooh, ginger beer,' said Jeff. 'I haven't had that for years. Are you going to try some, Sandy?'

Sandy nodded. Janet led them out to a patio and sat them down at a garden table. There was no wind and the sun was indeed warm for February. The garden stretched away to the stream; leaf-bare fruit trees marched down its length. A fountain splashed in a small pond. Bird feeders, fat balls and nut strings hung from the trees and there was a pair of binoculars on the table. They sat down whilst Janet bustled around in the kitchen, emerging soon carrying a tray with a tall jug and three glasses on it.

'Help yourself to home-made ginger beer. I'll go and get the cake.' She came back and put a large chocolate cake, glistening with dark chocolate icing, chocolate butter cream oozing from between the two layers, on the table. 'There,' she said, 'how does that look?'

'Lovely,' said Sandy politely.

'Mouth-watering!' said Jeff.

'I love baking,' Janet said. 'I made this for my friend Frances, who is coming over tomorrow. She can't eat all of it though!'

There was a flash of wings further down the garden and Janet picked up the binoculars and peered down the garden. She pointed at a tree near the boundary fence and said, 'See the woodpecker?' She showed Sandy how to focus the binoculars and Sandy looked where she pointed. 'It's a spotted woodpecker,' said Janet.

Sandy stared and then handed the binoculars to Jeff. 'It's amazing, Dad. Black and white and red. I didn't know there were birds like that in England!'

Janet laughed. 'Oh, we have plenty of colourful birds. I love the birds. In fact, it's one of the reasons why I don't want the cat in the garden. It would break my heart if he were to catch one and kill it.'

Sandy jumped up. 'Dad, I've had an idea! What about if Donko thinks he's a cat?'

Janet looked puzzled, and asked, 'Donko...?'

'Dad's a writer,' said Sandy. 'He writes the Donko books—'

Janet interrupted, 'Donko? Of course ... I remember Donko! The children at the library were always asking for those books and wondering when the next one was going to be coming.' She looked at Jeff. 'Fancy that. You're Jeff Grant then. I knew you were a writer but I didn't know you wrote those.'

Jeff grinned. 'Well, I'll be ... I'm always surprised when people know them. It was Sandy here who named him Donko.'

Sandy said, 'Dad's not been able to think of a new idea.' It had added to her worries. If he couldn't think because she was there he wouldn't be able to write, and then he wouldn't be able to earn any money and then he certainly wouldn't want her.

Jeff looked at her. 'How would that work then, Sandy? Donko being a cat?'

'It was that cat pouncing. I suddenly thought how funny the little dragon would look if he was doing that. And he could try and wash himself, only he'd set fire to himself wouldn't he?'

They all laughed, and Janet joined in with, 'He could try and curl up on someone's lap and purr. He could chase a piece of string and set fire to it!'

Jeff held out his arms to them both. 'Brilliant! Well done, Sandy! That's a marvellous idea. I'll get down to it this evening when you're tucked up in bed.' Jeff thought of the lies he had told his publisher and heaved a sigh of relief. Maybe he would get away with it.

They got up and Janet showed them back through the house. Sandy paused in the living room. She had never seen so many books in someone's house. 'Look at this, Dad. It's as good as a library!'

'Do you like reading?' asked Janet.

'Oh, I do,' Sandy replied.

'Well, would you like to come over by yourself one day and have a look? I'm sure there will be something you like. Why don't you come tomorrow morning? If that's fine with you, of course, Jeff.'

'I don't see why not. Would you like to, Sandy?'

Sandy had already pulled a book off a shelf and was engrossed in reading it. She looked up. 'Sorry. Yes, please,' she said, 'that would be great.'

Twenty

Lou was wakened by the ringing phone. Flyer sat up and stared at it, indignant. Nobody should interrupt their sleep. The clock hands pointed to seven a.m. Who on earth?

'Lou?'

'Jake! Is something wrong?'

'I'm in a muddle. I have to go out to a farm. One of the mares jumped wire in the night and has gashed herself badly. Alison is still away and Susie's school has an inset day. Could I dump her on you until tomorrow? The mare sounds really bad and I don't want Susie around if I have to put the poor beast down.'

'Of course you can. I'll take her shopping with me. I always take Janet on the first Thursday of the month. You know – the lady who's frightened of cats—'

Jake interrupted her. 'Sorry, Lou, but I must hurry. I'll see you in fifteen minutes.'

Lou showered, dressed and had a quick

breakfast of coffee and toast. Jake's car stopped outside, a car door slammed and Jake drove off without even coming in to say hello. Lou opened the door to greet Susie, taking her overnight bag from her and dumping it on the floor in the hall. Flyer greeted her with enthusiasm, weaving round her legs and yowling up at her.

Susie picked Flyer up and hugged him. 'I wish Daddy wasn't a vet,' she said.

'If wishes were horses then beggars would ride,' Lou said, remembering a saying of her grandmother's. 'We're going shopping and taking Miss Leigh. Have you had any breakfast yet?'

'Yes, thanks, I had some toast and a banana. Who's Miss Leigh?'

'She lives in The Bramble Patch next door. Don't you remember? I met her on the lane with Flyer when he was on a lead and she had a panic attack.'

'Is she still frightened of him?'

'I think she is. He never seems to go in her garden and I suspect she's chased him out. I've been taking her shopping for quite a few weeks now and she never says anything about him. I think she's embarrassed.'

'She sounds a bit weird.' Susie rubbed her cheek against Flyer's head and said, 'Fancy being frightened of you!'

'She's a lovely lady. You'll like her,' Lou said.

Janet was waiting for them, armed with a huge, black handbag and a shopping list. The bag made Lou laugh. 'It's big enough to carry an elephant in,' she had said when she first saw it.

'Could we call in at the library, just briefly?' Janet asked. 'A friend of mine's working there now. Frances told me. I'd love to see her.'

'Of course,' Lou replied and turned to Susie. 'Say hello to Miss Leigh—'

Janet interrupted her. 'Oh no. Not Miss, please. It makes me feel ninety! I'm Janet and you are...?'

'Susie,' Susie said, holding out a hand and surprising herself with her own formality.

Janet shook it and laughed. 'Pleased to meet you. Would you be the vet's daughter?'

Lou explained why she was there as they climbed into the car. Susie was enjoying herself. A day off school, a morning out shopping and a trip to the library. Maybe it wasn't so bad having a vet for a father. She wouldn't be here if he weren't. She gazed out of the window, watching for the first signs of spring. One of the houses on the way to Larksbridge stood on a grassy bank, which was always covered in snowdrops, and it thrilled her to see them. The first white buds were showing in the midst of milky-green spiked leaves, much to her delight. She pointed them out to Lou and Janet, both of them as pleased as she was.

Lou stopped in the library car park first. Inside, Janet breathed in the air and said, 'How it takes me back. Libraries always have a special smell. I don't know what it is.'

Lou grinned. 'I know what you mean! It's "eau de book"!'

A big woman with a mass of dark hair strode towards them. She grasped Janet's hands and said, 'How lovely to see you, Janet.' She hugged her and said, 'Just what the doctor ordered. I've been meaning to look you up for weeks. Listen, we have a story hour here every Saturday morning again. Is there any way you could come sometimes? The children used to love you reading to them. Now Frances doesn't do it, we're often short of volunteers. Do say yes!'

'I could bring her,' Lou said. 'And Susie too. I'm sure she'd love it, wouldn't you, sweetie?'

'What fun,' Susie said. 'I certainly would like to come sometimes. Perhaps I could help you choose the stories?' She giggled. 'I'll get to hear all my favourites then!'

By the end of the morning Janet was feeling somewhat bemused. She had enjoyed her shopping trip. Susie made even choosing food an adventure and had devised menus for both Lou and Janet, surprising them with foods that neither would have chosen. Shopping packed into the boot, they headed for home.

Janet turned round to Susie sitting in the back, and said, 'I can't believe some of the things I've bought. I'm really looking forward to eating them.'

Susie replied, 'Mum had lots of cookery books. I read them when I haven't anything else to read, only Dad won't let me do the cooking often. Mostly, if we don't have takeaways, Alison does it and what she serves up is soooo boring.'

Her face was a picture of disgust and Janet snorted with amusement. 'You want to be careful the north wind isn't blowing when you look like that!' she said. Her eyes lit up as she went on, 'You could both come and eat with me sometimes.' The thought of being of use again excited her.

'And why not you with me, for a change?' Lou said. 'Turn and turn about?'

Janet knew she couldn't do that. Not with Flyer in the house. That was asking too much. Even though, she realized, she owed the cat something. If it hadn't been for him Lou wouldn't have been out in the lane and she wouldn't be getting out and meeting all these people. And he had helped Sandy and Jeff in a funny sort of way!

Lou and Susie carried the bags into the house for Janet and Susie stared in amazement. She was enchanted. 'All those books,' she exclaimed, running over to the bookshelves.

'You like reading?' Janet asked.

'I love it. Only, we never have time to go to the library and it's too expensive to buy many. I spend my pocket money on them when I can.'

'How funny,' said Janet. 'You're the second person in a few days who has loved my books.'

'Who was the other one?' asked Susie.

'Strangely enough it was another girl – about your age, I think. She's called Sandy and lives with her dad down at The Twisted Willows.'

'Oh, is that who she is?' said Lou. 'I've seen them in passing but we've never stopped to chat. How awful, when we live so close.'

Susie could have spent hours browsing, but it was time to go.

Flyer still hated being alone. They heard his plaintive howls as they left Janet's house and he rushed to greet them when Lou opened the front door. Reunions sent him into such a delirium of delight he hardly knew what to do with himself. Rolling, rubbing, purring, yowling and begging to be picked up, he went through them all.

Lou knelt on the floor and he scrambled on to her lap. 'You,' she said, 'are nothing but a drama queen. Anyone would think you have been abandoned for days instead of hours.'

He shouted in agreement and butted his head under her chin. Lou laughed and put him down. 'Come on, Susie,' she said, 'Let's have some soup and those duck wraps for lunch, and then I must do some work. What do you want to do this afternoon?'

'I've got some homework to do and I'll play with Flyer. Perhaps he'll come outside with me for a bit.'

'OK,' said Lou. 'Do you want to work at the kitchen table?'

'I'd rather be in the dining room, if that's all right?'

'No problem,' said Lou. 'Just make sure that Flyer doesn't go into Janet's garden when you do go out.'

Lou tried to keep office hours for her work. It had always fascinated her and now she had several accounts from local farmers, the fish farm and some of the suppliers. Names became familiar, since the local farmers all used the same feed merchant. He supplied Lou with wholesale cat food and she did *his* accounts now too. Their regular accountant was over seventy and had been anxious to retire for some time, but none of his clients wanted – or needed – a big firm and he had stayed on reluctantly. He'd come to see Lou bearing, as well as his files, an enormous bunch of flowers. 'You're a godsend,' he'd said and, since he had said this to the farmers too, the nickname stuck.

'Is that our godsend?' asked the voices on the phone.

That was another source of interest for Flyer. He sat by Lou and tapped at the cord. He heard the voices that seemed to be hidden in the instrument.

She told Ray about the name and they decided that when she needed new business cards printed she would call herself 'Godsend Accountancy – Small Miracles a Speciality'. It made them both laugh and Ray said he had a friend who could come up with a design to go with it. 'A cat with wings and a halo,' he said jokingly.

'You could put a telephone in his paw,' she said. 'Jake rang once and I had to go and answer the doorbell. I put the receiver down and when I got back Flyer and Jake were having a long conversation down the phone! It was so funny ... Jake said I should use him as my secretary!'

That evening, after their tea, Susie asked, 'Can I have a bath before I go to bed? I love your bath. It's so big and it looks as if it might get up and walk away with me on those great big clawed feet!'

'Just watch out for Flyer, if you do. He likes to keep me company when I have one.' She laughed. 'He sits up by the taps and tries to catch the drips. His paws slipped one day and he fell in!'

Susie giggled and asked, 'What did he do?'

'It wasn't funny at the time. He used me as a springboard and jumped out so fast he was a blur! I have scars from the scratches he made,' she said ruefully. 'He knew he had lost his dignity. He turned his back on me and washed himself furiously for about ten minutes. Scarred for life, I am! So you watch out!'

'I will,' said Susie, grinning and patting Flyer who was sitting listening, knowing they were talking about him.

Lou got up and took the plates across to the dishwasher, and the butter back to the fridge. As soon as the door opened, Flyer was there, peering inside to see if there were any tasty morsels he could steal and shouting loudly about how hungry he was. She fed him three times a day and his internal clock seemed accurate to the minute. She always had lunch at midday, glad to escape her desk for an hour. Even if there was no sign of Flyer in house or garden, he would be bursting through the cat flap before the cuckoo had finished calling the hour and demanding his own meal with a barrage of noise.

'You,' Lou told him, 'are not a cat but a pig.'

'Or a Labrador cross,' Jake said one day when he heard her say it at a lunchtime visit. 'They are the greediest creatures.'

The atmosphere at the surgery was so unpleasant now that he often escaped to Lou at lunchtime. The three-mile drive was worth it. He brought sandwiches or a take-away, or she provided cold food: cooked chicken, ham or tinned salmon with salad. The hour's respite restored him and Lou missed him if he didn't come.

She knew he was unlikely to come today but he turned up after tea that evening when Susie was in bed.

'I'm at my wits' end,' Jake said. 'I finished surgery early and Alison turned up. She has been hanging around, pestering me with questions, yet again, offering to cook tea; lunch tomorrow—'

'Does she know you come here?' asked Lou.

'No. She and Christine think I go off to the pub for a pie and a pint.'

'She's besotted with you, Jake,' Lou said. 'Have you still not realized?'

'I need some peace and quiet and I seem to be surrounded by demanding women. But ... Alison can't be. I still can't believe it. It's ridiculous. She's only nineteen.'

'What on earth has that got to do with it?' Lou said, irritated with him. 'She never takes her eyes off you. And Susie realizes it. She knows you don't like Alison much and she's doing her best to help. Or so she thinks.'

'She's impossible at home. It just seems to be non-stop arguing. Maybe she is trying to help but it feels like it makes things worse.'

'Eleven is such an awful age,' said Lou. 'She's trapped in that horrible place where she's neither child, teenager nor adult. It's hard at the best of times and she probably feels as lost as you do.'

'Does she talk about it with you?' asked Jake.

'No, not really. I think she appreciates the space away from the surgery as much as you and she doesn't need to talk about it. She always seems happy here.'

Jake sighed and said, 'She does, doesn't she? Even I, insensitive as I apparently am, can see how different she is here. I wish...' He stopped.

'What?' said Lou. 'Wish what?'

'Nothing,' he muttered, embarrassed at what he had been about to say.

Lou got up and put her hand on his shoulder. 'You're a great father,' she said. 'So be patient with her. Just because it's hard doesn't mean you're getting it wrong. It just *is* hard sometimes.'

He placed his hand on hers, and glanced up at her. For a moment, they looked into each other's eyes and Lou, surprised by her feelings, turned away before she showed them.

Jake reluctantly let go and said, 'I want to get rid of Alison. But I can't sack the poor girl for falling in love with her boss, can I? None of the others can sleep in and I can't leave Susie alone at night, or take her with me.'

'I expect it will sort itself,' said Lou.

'God knows how,' said Jake with despair.

Twenty-One

Alison sighed. Holidays were very nice when they were happening but coming back always seemed so awful. The floor was filthy because of the rain and it looked as if everybody who'd come in had deliberately trodden in a mud puddle outside the door so that they could tramp it all over the waiting room floor. She'd have to get it clean before evening surgery started.

Feet pounded on the stair and Susie appeared in the doorway. She scowled at Alison and asked, 'Isn't Dad back yet?'

'No, he's not. He had to go out to the Jackson's farm and you know how far that is. He thought he would just make it back in time for surgery.'

'What am I going to have for tea?'

'Tea, is it? I thought you were feeling ill. I knew you should have gone to school this morning instead of hanging round here all day, getting in my way.'

Susie glared at her. 'I haven't been in your way. I've been in bed most of the day. And I did feel ill. I felt awful. I felt sick and my head hurt.' She stopped talking and sat down on one of the chairs, her face pale. 'If I could have gone to school, I would have done. It's my favourite lessons today.'

'Oh yeah?' said Alison, 'and what would they be?'

'I'm not telling you. It's none of your business.'

Alison picked up the mop and handed it to her. 'If you want some tea, you can clean the floor while I get it for you.'

'I'm not cleaning the floor. That's your job! I'll get my own tea,' shouted Susie.

'Fine!' said Alison, her temper rising. 'Suit yourself. How Jake could have such a horrible child, I do not know.'

Susie jumped to her feet, her eyes blazing.

'Maybe I am horrible, but Dad thinks you're horrible too. He hates you and he'll never, ever marry you. However much you want it.'

Neither of them heard the outer door open. Alison stepped across to Susie and slapped her hard across the face. She knew it was true but to hear it from Susie was too much. Susie gasped and put her hand to her cheek where the bright red imprint of Alison's hand stood out on her pale skin.

The door opened and Jake walked in. He stopped and took in the scene, his face thunderous. 'Alison, finish cleaning the floor. Susie, go to your room. I'll come and see you after surgery.'

He stamped off into the consulting room but Alison marched in after him. 'You can do surgery by yourself. I'm not staying another second in this place,' she said and stormed out, slamming the door behind her.

Jeff sighed and sat down.

'Shall I get you a cup of coffee, Dad?'

Jake looked up. Susie stood in the doorway, her eyes red from crying, her face still marked by Alison's hand.

'I'm sorry, Dad, but she was being really horrible and I lost my temper. What are you going to do without her?'

'Don't worry, sweetheart. We'll manage. Now go and get yourself cleaned up and looking respectable. We'll talk about it later.'

After surgery had finished, he looked in on Susie. She was asleep, the bedclothes tossed into a tangle around her. Jake sat down and stroked her hair. The pillow was wet. Her face looked flushed. He gently straightened the covers and, feeling a lump in one corner, he reached in and pulled out her old bear. She must be feeling bad for Harvey to have been retrieved from his usual place at the bottom of the wardrobe. There was no way she would be fit to go to school tomorrow. Perhaps Lou could have her for the day again.

Downstairs, he sat down and reached for the phone. Lou's number came without thought now and he willed her to answer. The phone rang and kept on ringing. He was just about to give up when she answered.

'Hello?'

'Lou? It's me, Jake.'

'Oh, hi. I was just off to bed. Is everything OK?'

'No, not really.' Jake felt exhausted. It all seemed a never-ending battle. If he had wanted to be a juggler he would have joined the circus. Life wasn't meant to be like this, was it?

'Jake? Come on, what's happened?'

'Oh, well, the little problem of Alison seems to have resolved itself. I got back to find her and Susie having the most tremendous row, which ended in Alison slapping Susie. I didn't actually sack her because she did it herself. Now I've got nobody to help tomorrow and Susie looks terrible. She could do with a day off school tomorrow.'

'I'll come over and get her first thing then. She can spend the day with me. You know she's always welcome here.'

'Oh, thanks, Lou –' he breathed a sigh of relief – 'what would I do without you?'

'Don't be daft, man. You go and get yourself some sleep and I'll see you in the morning.'

Janet bundled the last of her washing into the laundry basket and reached for the peg bag hanging on the hook by the back door. She hated those winter days when she knew that hanging the washing in the garden was nothing but wishful thinking; today though the sun shone and a breeze blew ragged grey clouds across the sky. It was true that frost gleamed white in the shaded areas but the day was full of promise. Snowdrops in the borders fluttered and the first green spikes of the daffodil leaves were pushing up through the earth.

What had Arthur said all those months ago?

'Never give up hope, lass.'

He had been right.

How much fuller her life was now. She called in to see him sometimes, enjoying the reminiscences of the old days and the tales he had to tell from his days in the Navy. Frances came round once a month and Lou often dropped in to say hello or to take her out somewhere. Sandy called in to borrow books and she had even persuaded Janet to play French cricket with her once! The morning of storytelling at the library had been magical and she felt as though a hidden fairy had waved a wand over her life.

It would be perfect if it wasn't for the cat, Flyer. She still eyed him warily when he crouched at the edge of her garden. Everybody else adored him. She wished she could too.

Janet walked down the garden to the clothesline, stretched between two pear trees.

Down at the far end, where the little,

wooden bridge crossed the stream, she had had a small pond dug out. A tumble of stones edged it and in the summer ferns sprouted between them, loving the shade they found there.

Janet put her laundry basket down and began to peg, humming softly as she went. The basket empty, she turned to admire the washing fluttering in the wind. She decided to go down towards the stream, look out over the fields beyond and see what the rest of the world was up to. In the shade it was cool after the sun and she shivered. A small, yellow flower in a nest of green between the stones and the margin of the pond caught her eye. Had primroses seeded themselves there?

She stepped on to a stone to see better. It was still icy and her foot went from under her. It slipped between two stones and she fell heavily, her foot trapped. She screamed out in agony and fainted. Flyer, next door, pricked his ears.

Janet came to, lying cold, sick and shaken, sprawled on the stones. She struggled to get to her feet. She couldn't do it. It was agony trying to pull her foot from between the stones. To make matters worse, the fall had twisted her bad knee. Blood welled in the palms of her hands where she had cut them as she fell and one wrist throbbed painfully. Moving was out of the question.

Weakly, she called out but she was a long way down the garden and there was nobody about. She closed her eyes and wondered what on earth to do. How could she make anybody hear? Clouds had blotted out the sun and she couldn't stop shivering. She tried her usual remedy when she felt powerless. 'Come on, pull yourself together, Janet,' she said crossly, out loud.

It didn't work.

The first flakes of snow began to fall, drifting downwards to settle on her already cold face and to speckle her navy jacket with white. She shouted again, trying to put in every ounce of energy she had. It sounded feeble and she groaned. *How silly*, she thought, *to die at the bottom of my own garden*. If only she could make someone hear.

There was a soft touch on her face and she opened her eyes, imagining it was a bigger snowflake. Instead, she saw Flyer, his blue eyes staring at her. He reached out a dark paw again and touched her gently on the cheek.

Flyer could smell her fear, smell the pain and the blood on her cut hands, and recognized it as a memory of his own drama. He had heard her scream and come to investigate.

Tentatively, Janet reached out a hand and stroked his head. He purred. 'Hello, Flyer,' she said. 'You haven't abandoned me then, after all the horrid things I've said about you.' His tongue rasped on her wrist and she stroked him again. 'I need you to help me, Flyer,' she whispered and tried to sit up. The pain made her gasp and Flyer yowled. He yowled again, his raucous shouts filling the air but still nobody came.

'You'll have to go and find somebody,' said Janet. 'Please, Flyer.' She wished he were a dog. That was the sort of thing you heard about dogs doing. But a cat? Surely not. Flyer bounded off up the garden, shouting loudly. Janet crossed her fingers. Perhaps he would get somebody.

Next door, Susie was making buns in the kitchen. The cat flap rattled and Flyer dived through, coming in like a torpedo. He skidded across the floor and stooped beside Susie. His shouts filled the kitchen and she laughed at him. 'Good grief, cat, what a racket.'

He rubbed round her legs, yelling at the top of his voice and she bent to pick him up.

'You have got a tale to tell. Are there monsters in the garden that you want me to know about?'

Flyer wriggled out of her arms and jumped to the floor. He ran to the back door, looking back at her.

'You do want to show me something. What is it, Flyer?'

He pushed back through the cat flap and she opened the door to follow him, astonished to see the snow falling. What was he up to? He usually hated being out in it.

He led her out of Lou's front garden down the road and into Janet's garden, calling anxiously and turning to make sure she was following.

Susie shouted, 'No, Flyer not in there. You know Janet is frightened of you.'

The cat ignored her admonitions and ran round the side of the house. Susie followed and heard a faint shout. She stopped and listened. There it was again, coming from the bottom of the garden.

There was another raucous yowl from Flyer and he raced down the garden, past the washing flapping on the line. Susie rushed after him, catching the urgency. She saw Janet, lying on the stones by the pond, Flyer beside her.

Janet was laughing and crying. 'You clever cat.' Her hand stroked his head and Flyer yowled and licked her hand.

Susie ran up to her. 'Janet! What have you done to yourself?'

'Oh, Susie, thank goodness you've come. I think I've broken my ankle.'

Susie squatted down and took her hand. 'You'll be all right. I'll go and get some blankets to keep you warm and we'll phone for an ambulance.' She patted Flyer and said. 'You stay here and look after her.' She raced back, terrified for Janet. She was so cold, her teeth chattering, face and hands blue.

Lou looked up from her accounts when Susie shouted, panic in her voice, 'Lou? Lou? You've got to come now. Janet's fallen in the garden and broken her ankle. And it's snowing. Flyer found her and came to tell me.'

Lou jumped up and ran through to the kitchen. 'Where is she?'

'At the bottom of her garden. We'll have to get an ambulance for her. Have you got any blankets to keep her warm?'

Lou grabbed the phone and dialled 999. A voice spoke and she told them what had happened. 'Look in the chest on the landing,' she shouted to Susie. 'There're some old blankets in there.'

Susie dashed upstairs and came down clutching two old green blankets under one arm, a pillow under the other. 'I'll take these out now.'

When they got back to Janet, Flyer was curled up beside her and they were having a long conversation.

Lou squatted beside her and took her hand. Janet grimaced and Lou let go quickly. 'Oh, Janet, poor, poor you. What have you done to yourself?'

'I think I've broken my ankle and sprained my wrist,' Janet whispered. 'I'm so cold, Lou.'

Lou took the blankets from Susie and tucked them carefully round her. 'At least these will keep the snow and wind off you. I've phoned for an ambulance and they'll be here in ten minutes.'

Janet grimaced and said weakly, 'I might be dead by then.'

'No, you won't,' Lou said briskly. 'How come Flyer found you?'

'He must have heard me scream. He hasn't come in my garden for ages. Not since I chased him away. If it hadn't been for him I would have been here all day. I really might have died, mightn't I?' Fear and shock overwhelmed her and she began to weep. Flyer rubbed his face against hers and licked the end of her nose.

'He looks like he's taking good care of you now,' said Lou, rubbing Janet's good hand vigorously under the blanket, trying to warm her.

Janet, recovering a little, said, 'It seems so silly to think of how frightened I have been of him. From devil to saviour in the space of five minutes!'

Lou smiled. 'He's a very special cat, that one.' She tucked the blankets around Janet again and said, 'Isn't that the siren? The ambulance is here. I'll go to the hospital with you. Susie, can you run up and show them where to come?'

Janet said, 'Mind you don't fall!'

'I'll be careful,' Susie shouted over her shoulder as she ran off.

Ten minutes later, Janet was safely into the ambulance, Lou beside her and Flyer back in the house. For once he didn't protest at being left, sensing the need.

'Can I come too?' asked Susie.

'No, I think it would be better if you didn't. We could be hours.' She thought for a moment. 'I know! We can drop you off at the farm where I get the eggs and milk. You know the Laytons, don't you? And it's on the way to the hospital.'

'Oh, yes,' said Susie. 'I've been there with Dad. They've got a pig that has just farrowed.'

After the ambulance had dropped her off, Susie watched it disappear down the track from the farm.

Trish came out to meet her. 'What's happening? Lou didn't say much when she rang except that it was an emergency. Is she all right?'

'Oh, yes, she's fine. It's her neighbour, Janet. She fell over and broke her ankle. Flyer's a hero because he found her and came to tell me about her. She could have been there all night otherwise.' Susie shuddered. It didn't bear thinking about – not in the snow that was still falling, blanketing the ground.

'You come in and have a mug of hot chocolate. That's your favourite, isn't it? There are some scones in the oven and there's somebody I'd like you to meet.'

Susie walked into the kitchen and a small figure sitting at the table turned to look at her.

'This is Sandy,' said Tricia. 'Her dad's Jeff who lives down at the end of the lane where Lou lives, and she's spending the day with us too.'

Susie smiled. 'Hello, Sandy. I've heard of you. Janet says you like books!'

The girl smiled back. 'Hello, I do. How do you know Janet?'

Susie explained and Sandy said, 'Fancy! All those months and we have been nearly next door to one another sometimes! Would you like to see my donkey?'

'Oh wow,' said Susie. 'Your own donkey? Yes, please.'

Sandy turned to Trish and said anxiously, 'Is that all right?'

'Of course it is. Just wrap up warm against the snow and come back in ten minutes for that drink and scones. Don't let yourselves get too cold.'

The girls went out and Sandy pulled her across the yard, excited at having a friend to show off Amelia to. They raced across the yard, trying to catch snowflakes on their tongues and laughing when they did. In the next field they headed up to the shed and Sandy carefully opened the door. A small, grey donkey came over and nuzzled up against Sandy, trying to get her nose into her coat pocket.

Sandy laughed. 'This is Amelia,' she said. 'Isn't she sweet?'

She took out some pieces of apple and offered them to the little animal, who sniffed and took them delicately. They patted and fussed the little creature, oblivious of the time, until finally they said goodbye and closed the door on her.

'Shall we go and see the new piglets on the way back?' said Sandy.

'Oh, yes, they're only a couple of days old, aren't they?'

They leaned over the sty door and didn't notice Trish coming across the yard, wondering what had happened to them both.

Sandy said, 'The first time I saw piglets here was just after my mum died. She'd been ill for months and we came over from America so I could live with Dad. That's when Trish and Ben said I could have the baby donkey when it was born – only living here, not with me.'

Susie turned to look at her. 'My mum died two years ago.'

'Do you live with your dad then?' asked Sandy.

'Yes. He's the vet which is why I knew about the piglets.'

'My dad's a writer. I have to be very careful not to annoy him because if I do I'll be sent away. That's what one of the social workers said.'

Trish heard these last words and was horrified. Poor child! No wonder she was so well behaved. She coughed and the girls turned. 'Your turn for a go at the milk bar,' she laughed. 'But I think I have something a bit more exciting to offer than sow's milk!'

'Ooh, yummy,' said Susie. 'Is it my favourite? Scones with jam and cream?'

'It certainly is. And marshmallows to float on your chocolate if you want. Come on.'

She left the girls in the kitchen, chatting and playing with the dogs, and went off to phone Jeff. He needed to know about Sandy's fears. 'Jeff? Is that you? Sorry to bother you, but there's something you need to know.' She recounted what Sandy had said.

Jeff groaned. 'Bloody social workers. They are supposed to help and it seems to me they make things harder sometimes. How could anybody be so insensitive? Thanks for telling me, Trish. I'll talk to Sandy.'

Almost as soon as Trish put the phone down it rang again, and she picked it up. 'Lou's back from the hospital,' she said to the girls, once she'd finished with the call. 'I'm going to take you both over there and Jeff will pick you up from Lou's, Sandy. OK?'

'Yeah, sure,' they both said.

Lou greeted them both at the door. 'Hello, Sandy, I'm pleased to meet you at last. Have you both had a good day? Janet's going to be fine. They're going to operate on her ankle tomorrow. Her wrist is sprained badly but not broken, and she'll be in hospital for about a week.' She laughed. 'She asked me to buy a fillet of salmon as a gift from her for Flyer, so I did. Look at him.'

The cat was crouched over a plate of fish, purring loudly enough to drown out the sound of the cuckoo popping out to announce the time.

Sandy was entranced. 'I've met him before. He was outside Janet's house when Dad and I lost our ball. Janet hates him, doesn't she?'

'Not any more,' said Susie. 'He saved her today. If it hadn't been for him, Janet might still be lying in her back garden in all this snow.'

'Come and sit here,' said Lou. 'He'll want a lap to sit on after he's eaten that lot. I'm sure he'll be happy to sit on yours.'

Sandy sat and waited. Flyer finished eating and sat up licking his lips, making sure that not one tasty little morsel had escaped. He looked round and yowled.

'He's saying that was nice,' said Sandy. She patted her lap and to her delight the cat jumped up, turned round three times and settled down on her knee. He half-heartedly licked one paw.

'He's too full to wash himself,' said Susie.

Sandy stroked his head and Flyer purred loudly.

The doorbell rang and they jumped. 'That'll be your dad,' said Lou and went to open the door. Jeff stepped in.

'Oh, hi, Dad. Look who I've met today. This is Susie and this is Flyer.'

'Are you ready to come home yet?' said Jeff.

'No, not really,' said Sandy. She gasped, bit her lower lip and then looked down.

'Of course I'm ready, Daddy. I'll come now,' she said, head bent. She placed Flyer on the floor and stood up, her eyes still on the floor.

Jeff knelt in front of her. He had been going to have a quiet talk with her in private but this couldn't wait. Her expression was breaking his heart. He squatted down and took her gently by the shoulders. 'Look at me, Sandy,' he said.

She lifted her eyes and looked at him, wondering what on earth he was going to say. Was this it? The moment when he sent her back because she had argued? Her eyes filled with tears and her dad pulled her to him.

'Trish told me what you said, about the social worker saying I would send you away if you weren't good.'

Sandy looked up at him. Yes, this was going to be the moment when her fears came true.

'The only person who is going to be sent away is that social worker,' said Jeff. 'You and I are together forever. And you can be as naughty as you like. Do you hear me, Sandy?'

She looked at him and whispered, 'Yes.' Then she grinned and said, 'Naughty how?'

Jeff laughed and stood up. 'You use your imagination, my girl. I know you have plenty of that. Now, are you coming home or do you want to stay a bit longer?'

'I'd like to stay.'

Lou smiled. 'Good. No problem. Why don't you all stay and have some lunch with us?'

Sandy pouted. 'But I can't be naughty if you've given us all permission to stay. I want them to go!'

Everybody burst out laughing and Flyer joined in with a raucous meow.

Twenty-Two

Lou looked round the room, checking that everything was there. She hoped Janet would be comfortable. It wasn't perfect but it was the best that could be managed. She and Frances had met up whilst visiting Janet in hospital and come up with the plan. There was no way that Janet could manage by herself in her own house and at least Lou had a downstairs toilet and shower. It would only be for a few weeks until Janet had her strength and mobility back.

Flowered curtains fluttered at the window and a shaft of sunlight spread across the patchwork quilt on the bed. Flyer was curled up on the cover purring in the warmth from the sun and washing his face. Waiting for his protégée to come home!

From the kitchen the cuckoo called three times and Lou turned and hurried downstairs. Just a bunch of flowers to be picked and put on the window sill and then she could go and get Janet, and get her settled before she and Jake went out tonight.

Janet had been firm that they go. 'Of course you can go out, Lou. Don't be silly. I'll be fine. I can watch the television and luxuriate in being able to do what I want when I want. Susie will look after me.' She was adamant. 'It's your birthday and you're going.'

She'd surprised herself. Janet Leigh? Being bossy?

In Lou's own room a new dress hung, ready for her date tonight with Jake. It was aquamarine and floaty; she felt like a glamour queen when she wore it, along with strappy sandals with heels. She'd bought a pale blue shrug to go with it. How she was looking forward to tonight. It seemed centuries since she had had a glamorous evening out.

Cards lined the mantelpiece and she paused to look at them. So many friends remembering her birthday. Johnny's photograph stood in its usual place on the mantelpiece and she picked it up. It still hurt but it was like the vicar had said. 'You had to wait for life to take you into another room.' She laughed. Flyer had been the train! He sounded like one, sometimes.

'Come on Lou, time to go,' she said to herself and replaced Johnny's photograph carefully, grabbed the car keys and her bag and headed out to fetch Janet from the hospital.

Jake picked her up at six thirty. Janet and Susie were watching a cookery programme and waved them off cheerfully. Jake stuck his head round the door and winked at Janet while Lou was getting in the car. She grinned at him and gave a thumbs up sign. 'How long do you need?' he asked.

'Give us an hour and a half. The troops are ready to roll in as soon as you've disappeared round the corner. Now, off you go and have fun!'

The horn beeped from outside and Jake said, 'I'd better go. Madam is getting impatient.'

'Bye! See you later!'

As soon as he'd gone and the car had turned out of the drive Janet whispered, 'You can come out now, Sandy.'

From behind the settee, Sandy crawled

out, giggling. 'That was so funny. I was sure I was going to sneeze or something.'

'I thought I would laugh too. Now, what do you want me to do?'

'Can you blow up the balloons and tie them into bunches with this?' She handed Janet two plastic bags of brightly-coloured balloons and a spool of silver ribbon.

'I'll explode blowing all those up!'

'No, you won't. We've got you a balloon pump! Do you want a cup of tea while you do it?'

'Sounds good to me,' said Janet as she ripped open the packet.

'I'm going to get the table ready for all the food,' said Susie. 'I'll be back in a few minutes.'

A car rolled into the drive and Meg and Grace from the transport café emerged from it. They opened the boot and started pulling out box after box. A battered old Ford soon pulled up behind their car and Janet's friends Frances and Arthur climbed out, both clutching huge bunches of flowers.

In the wine bar the after work crowd were celebrating the end of the week. It was happy hour and Lou was drinking from a tall cocktail glass adorned with a little paper umbrella and a cherry. It was bright orange layered with red and it was delicious. Jake had his usual pint. He put down the glass and looked at Lou.

Lou smiled at him. 'What's up? You look like Susie with something to say.'

Jake laughed. 'Well, I do have something to say. Something to ask you, in fact.' He pulled a little blue-velvet box out of his pocket and said, 'This is your birthday present, Lou.' He reached into the other pocket and pulled out an envelope. 'There's this to go with it. I've been wanting to ask you for ages.' He handed them both to her saying, 'I wanted you to have the ring because...' He was lost for words.

Lou opened the dark-blue velvet box. Inside a platinum ring, woven into a Celtic knot, lay in a white-silk nest. 'Oh, Jake, it's beautiful. Thank you. What's in the envelope?' He blushed and she laughed. 'Come on, Jake. Talk to me.'

He put his hand over hers and said, 'Lou, I want to ask you if you'd consider marrying me. I know it might be too soon after Johnny for you, and maybe too soon for me. So this ring is like a promise between us that we're going to go on together and see where we get to. But the envelope...' He opened it and handed her three air tickets. 'Susie and I wondered if you would come on holiday with us – in September.'

Lou looked at him and at the ring. She blinked back tears and put a hand over his. 'Well, the answer is yes! Oh Jake, I can't believe it. What a lovely birthday present.'

Jake took her hand and looked at it. The rings from her marriage to Johnny were still there.

She took them off and put them on her right hand. 'Jake, you know what? I don't need to wait. I knew Johnny was right for me, I knew Flyer was what I needed and I have the same knowing about you. I'll wear this ring on my engagement finger. I don't want to stop wearing the others. They're too much a part of me and Johnny always will be. But this is beautiful.'

She held out her left hand and he slipped the ring on to her finger. It was a perfect fit. 'You cunning old devil. How did you do that?' she asked.

He smiled proudly. 'Oh, it was easy. I borrowed one of your dress rings. Susie found it for me.'

'Does she know you were going to propose?'

'Yes. I didn't feel like I could do it without her being OK about it.'

'And was she?'

'Er, I think ecstatic would just about describe her reaction.'

Lou smiled. 'Good, that just about describes mine too. But what will we do about Flyer when we're away? And what about the practice?'

Jake grinned. 'I had a good day yesterday. Someone applied for the vacancy and I've met up with him. We like each other and he's starting next month. It means I'll have time to get him going and then leave him to it!'

Lou said, 'Oh great. I'm so pleased.' She giggled, 'Perhaps Janet will feed Flyer now. I think she's going to be his willing slave!'

Jake said, 'Our table is booked for half an hour's time. We'd better go.' He reached into his pocket and frowned. 'That's funny. Where's my wallet?' He clapped a hand to his forehead. 'Oh no. Remember I pulled it out when we were at your place to get a business card out? I've left it in the living room. I'm sorry, Lou, We'll have to go back for it. I've got just enough to pay for these drinks and that's all.'

'Can't I pay?'

'No, certainly not. Not on your birthday. It won't take long and we can check up on Janet at the same time.'

They heard the engine as the car pulled into the lane and Jeff shouted, 'Action stations!' People disappeared like magic – Susie and Sandy behind the settee; Jeff into the bathroom; Janet hobbled into the kitchen with Meg and Grace lending a supporting hand on either side, Frances and Arthur giggling behind them. Trish and Ben sneaked into the hall cupboard, hysterical because they could hardly shut the door. Ray, in a panic, dashed upstairs to lurk on the landing, a man wearing a clerical collar chasing after him.

A car door slammed and they heard Lou say, 'Oh, look. One of the girls has tied a birthday balloon to the gate for me. That's nice. I wonder when they did it?'

The front door opened and Flyer came to meet them. He had no idea what was going on but whatever it was, was fun. All sorts of tasty little tit bits had come his way and he hoped for more. He curved in and out between Lou's legs purring loudly and yowling. She bent to pick him up. 'What's the matter with you?'

Lou stood up and nearly dropped Flyer when the bathroom door burst open and Jeff bellowed, 'Now!'

Suddenly there were people everywhere all shouting, 'Surprise, surprise. Happy birthday, Lou! Happy birthday!'

For a moment she was overwhelmed – then a grin split her face from ear to ear. 'What a plotter you are,' she said to Jake and prodded him in the ribs. He grinned.

Susie shouted, 'Come and see the table, Lou.'

The dining room table was piled with plates of food. Everybody had brought something, as well as the feast that Meg and Grace had brought with them. Balloons hung from the ends of the curtain poles, from the window latches, from the book shelves. A huge banner went across one wall, 'Happy Birthday' printed in bright-red letters edged with gold. There were vases of flowers everywhere.

Susie went up and whispered in Jake's ear, 'Do we need the other one, Dad?'

He nodded and she yelled, 'Yes!' at the top of her voice and reached under the table to pull out a second banner. 'Help me with it, Sandy,' she said and the two girls pinned it up on the other wall. 'Congratulations on your engagement, Jake and Lou,' it said, in bright golden letters.

Everybody cheered and Lou felt as if her heart would burst with happiness. She stared in amazement as the vicar from Johnny's memorial service stepped forwards. Lou ran over and hugged him, tears in her eyes. 'I can't believe you're here, Andrew,' she said. 'How on earth...?'

He grinned and said, 'That's a devious man you have attached yourself to. Vet and detective, I think.'

Lou stepped back holding both his hands. She let go of one and put a hand to her cheek. 'That was some ticket you gave me,' she said. 'I wonder if you would marry Jake and me?'

He smiled and said with great sincerity, 'Nothing would give me greater pleasure, Lou.'

Susie hugged her tight and she and Janet smiled at each other over her head. Flyer jumped on the table to see what he fancied. Everybody was too busy to notice him.

At that moment, the doorbell rang.

Ray said, 'Oh, I hope you don't mind, Lou. That'll be my new girlfriend. I wanted you to meet her and she said her father wants a new accountant. He's brought her so that he knows where you live.'

'Of course I don't mind,' said Lou. 'The more the merrier.'

Meg went to open it. A big man with dark hair stood on the doorstep, a child beside him with a halo of blonde curls and a young woman who looked like a grown up version of the little girl beside him.

'Hi,' the young woman said. 'I'm Sara. This is Zannie and my dad, Mark.'

'Hello,' Mark said. 'I know it's not a good time to call. We've just come to drop Sara off. I can come back another time.

'Oh no,' said Meg reaching for his hand and pulling him in. 'Now's a perfect time. Come and join in the fun. Lou knows you're coming and wants you to join the party.'

'Well, all right. Just for a minute then. I do want to see Lou about doing our farm accounts but that can wait.'

Zannie jumped up and down with excitement. 'Ooh, goody! I love parties!'

Ray came through from the kitchen. He kissed Sara and said, 'Hello, darling.' He slapped Mark on the shoulder and tousled Zannie's hair. 'Hi there. How're you?'

Lou came over and said, 'Come in and have a drink, something to eat. We're just about to attack the food mountain.' She peeped into the dining room. 'Uh, oh! Someone's got there first.'

Flyer was sitting in the middle of the table, a piece of chicken dangling from his mouth. He had the grace to look guilty.

Zannie stopped and stared. He looked at her and a slow purr rumbled deep in his throat. It turned into a crescendo of excited yells and he leapt straight into her arms, rubbing his head ecstatically against her face.

'Flyer?' she shouted. 'It's Flyer! I know it's Flyer!'

'Well, I'll be darned,' said Mark. 'So it is! I can't believe it. We were afraid he might be dead.'

'Come and sit down and I'll tell you the story,' said Lou, leading them back to the settee.

They listened in amazement. Lou finally stopped for breath. 'And that's about it, really. He's been a little miracle for all of us in his own way. None of these people would be here or know each other if it hadn't been for him.' She stopped and looked at Zannie, her face buried in the cat's fur. 'Of course, he's your cat really. If you want to take him back then I'll understand.'

Mark looked at Zannie and said, 'What do

you think? It's up to you.'

Zannie looked round at everybody and said slowly, 'I did miss him but I think it's enough to know he's OK. Like you said he would be, Daddy. That he hadn't used up all his lives and he would find a new home.' She thought for a moment then went on, 'I think he belongs here with these people. He's their "forever" cat now. If you have your accounts done here I can come and visit Flyer, can't I, Daddy?'

Lou hugged her. 'Of course you can, Zannie. You'll always be welcome.'

Zannie looked up at her father and said, 'He's brought them all luck, hasn't he, Daddy?'